"Please, Mr. Slader, I need your help."

Why did she have to go and say that? He had to make her understand she didn't belong in the Amazon. She was as much out of place as a snowman would be. "I can't help you. You need to get on the first boat out of here and return to wherever you came from."

"I can't go home until I find my brother. If you can't help me, I'll have to find someone else who will."

Slader leaned forward, getting a whiff of perfume that smelled like the rose garden his— He shook the memory from his mind. He never walked down that path. Ever. "Lady, there is no one else."

"Then you have to help me or..." Kate searched for words, her perfect white teeth nibbling her bottom lip.

"Or what?"

"I'll search on my own."

Books by Margaret Daley

Love Inspired Suspense

Hearts on the Line #23
Heart of the Amazon #37

Love Inspired

The Power of Love #168
Family for Keeps #183
Sadie's Hero #191
The Courage to Dream #205
What the Heart Knows #236
A Family for Tory #245
*Gold in the Fire #273
*A Mother for Cindy #283

*Light in the Storm #297
The Cinderella Plan #320
*When Dreams Come True #339
*Tidings of Joy #369

*The Ladies of Sweetwater Lake

MARGARET DALEY

feels she has been blessed. She has been married more than thirty years to her husband, Mike, whom she met in college. He is a terrific support and her best friend. They have one son, Shaun. Margaret has been writing for many years and loves to tell a story. When she was a little girl, she would play with her dolls and make up stories about their lives. Now she writes these stories down. She especially enjoys weaving stories about families and how faith in God can sustain a person when things get tough. When she isn't writing, she is fortunate to be a teacher for students with special needs. Margaret has taught for over twenty years and loves working with her students. She has also been a Special Olympics coach and participated in many sports with her students.

HEART OF THE
AMAZON

MARGARET DALEY

Steeple
Hill®

Published by Steeple Hill Books™

STEEPLE HILL BOOKS

Steeple
Hill®

ISBN-13: 978-0-373-87413-2
ISBN-10:   0-373-87413-8

HEART OF THE AMAZON

www.SteepleHill.com

Printed in U.S.A.

Draw near to God and He will draw near to you.
—*James* 4:8

To the man I love, my husband, Mike

ONE

Hot, humid—no, make that wet—air clung to her like a second skin. Kate Collier dabbed a tissue along her brow, over her cheeks, then her upper lip. The second she stuffed the tissue back into her black purse, perspiration popped out on her face again, putting a new layer of dampness on top of the old.

Where is the Blue Dolphin?

She scanned the street—if she could call the pothole-riddled single lane of packed dirt a street. She was beginning to think she needed a guide to find the guide the hotel had given her directions to over a half an hour ago. It wasn't as though this place was a major city. Probably no more than two thousand lived here, if that. But she had wandered the streets of Mandras, Brazil, and was going to have to admit she was lost. Like her brother. That thought spurred her on. She needed help.

Turning the corner, going farther away from the more civilized parts of Mandras—and that was a generous usage of the word *civilized*—she saw the sign at an angle, barely held up by a rusted chain at one end. *Blue Dolphin Bar.* Bar? The hotel hadn't said anything about her going into a bar.

Oh, my! This would never do!

She stood outside the seedy-looking building that had patches of what had once been yellow paint still clinging to parts of the wooden structure. It housed a bar on its lower floor, and she wasn't sure she really wanted to know what was in the top story. She gnawed on her bottom lip while she tried to decide what to do. She had never been in a bar in her whole thirty-eight years. Never. Not once. If she went inside, she could imagine the horror on the faces of the people back home at the church where she was the secretary if they knew. She could imagine the horror on her own face!

She fortified herself with a deep breath and nearly choked on the scent of rotting fish and decaying plants with just a hint of stale…beer? Releasing the breath, she hiked the strap of her purse up on her shoulder and hugged it close to her. From inside, the sounds of loud voices and laughter drifted out to her. The man called Slader, according to not just the manager at the hotel, but anyone else she had contacted, was the only one who would take her to where she needed to go. She had no choice.

Lord, please protect and guide me. Tell me what I should do. I have to find my brother. I know he isn't dead. Please help me to get through the next few minutes—alive!

Still undecided, Kate scanned the area and realized for the first time that there were not many people out and about, which made her situation even more precarious. Being in the middle of the afternoon, there was little traffic on the street and certainly not anything that looked even remotely like a taxi to take her back to her hotel. And worse, not far from this street she could see the river and jungle, a wall of various shades of green with a ribbon of brown running through it.

A group of men, all scruffy looking, as though they had just been let out of prison, suddenly exited a tin-roofed building across the street and headed toward her en masse. Her heart began to pound so fast that the images before her tilted and spun. Clutching the post next to her, she squeezed her eyes closed for a few seconds, hoping she was seeing things that weren't there.

Someone jostled her, sending her into the main stream of men. Their rancid odor, a mixture of sweat, unwashed bodies and something unidentifiable, engulfed her. Her eyes snapped open. Someone else bumped into her from behind. Before she realized what was happening, the eight men swept her along with them into the bar, their cackles and snickering remarks causing her ears to burn. Thankfully she had no idea what they were saying, since she didn't speak Portuguese, or more than her ears would be burning. Which brought her to another problem. What if no one spoke English? How would she find Mr. Slader, especially if he wasn't here?

"Excuse me," she squeaked out to the nearest man.

He twisted around and glared at her.

Her mind went blank while her full attention glued

itself to the long, ugly red scar that slashed down his face from hairline to chin.

"What's a lady like you doing here?" one of the other men said in broken English, followed by some more Portuguese, then a round of laughter, the deep belly kind, as though she was the punch line of a joke.

Heat that had nothing to do with the soaring tropical temperature scored her cheeks, even though now that she was away from the scorching sun it was cooler in the bar by a few degrees. She started to speak to the man who had spoken a semblance of English, but visions of her foolhardiness for even being in this place flashed before her. Nothing would come out of her mouth.

The men parted and ambled toward the scarred bar to order their drinks or to join others at the tables scattered around the room. Several threw her one last look and dismissed her as unimportant—probably downright unattractive, therefore not worth their time.

Left alone in the middle of the bar, she bristled at how they had walked away. Didn't they see she needed help? That thought brought her up short. She hadn't wanted their attention, so why was she upset at not getting it?

Kate, you are losing it. You are definitely out of your element. She should have been ecstatic that she was plain and unappealing to men. But still, what was she going to do about finding Mr. Slader without assistance?

Ignoring her lapse in logic, she went about doing what she had set out to do with or without anyone's help—find Mr. Slader and hire him as her guide. In the dim light she surveyed the patrons of the bar, trying to decide which one was the man in question, that was if he was even at the bar. But the hotel manager had claimed that Mr. Slader would be here *if* he was in town. She'd thought the manager had meant this was Mr. Slader's office and the Blue Dolphin was the name of the building or even the name of another hotel. What a mistake!

Then she saw the man who had to be Mr. Slader, from the manager's description, at the end of the long bar that ran the length of the room. He toyed with a glass full of a golden brown liquid, never picking it up. Lifting his gaze, he stabbed her with penetratingly dark eyes that bored into her and nearly pinned her to the swinging doors several feet behind her, such was the power behind his regard.

With all the courage she could muster—which she decided was puny at best—she started forward, caught in his snare. He straightened when she headed toward him, a deep frown carving lines into his tanned features. That movement pulled her attention to the breadth of his wide shoulders and the muscular arms that rested on the counter. The manager had said he was a large man, but that description really didn't depict him adequately.

When her focus returned to that face hardened by the sun's rays, she gasped at the arch of his brow and the amusement lighting the dark brown depths of his eyes. He cocked his head and turned slightly. That was when she lit upon the scar that ran from his left ear across part of his cheek. It conveyed a toughness that she wasn't used to.

He was the second man with a scar whom she had seen in the past five minutes. In the heat she shivered and, by the lift of his eyebrow, knew he had seen her reaction. The amusement in his expression grew.

Please let me be wrong. Don't let him be Mr. Slader.

The bar's constant noise decreased in volume to a few murmurs. Most of the patrons paused and waited to see what transpired at the end of the bar, between her and the man with black hair longer than hers pulled back and tied with a leather strap. She caught a sympathetic look in one man's eyes that sent panic bolting through her.

Run now before it's too late, her sensible side screamed. Then she remembered her brother and knew she couldn't, no matter that every alarm bell in her mind pealed a deafening toll.

Why did Mr. Slader have to be the only guide available?

She should have asked the hotel manager why he insisted Mr. Slader was the only one available, but in her eagerness to begin her search for her brother, she'd flown out of the shabby lobby and in the direction the man had indicated, only remembering fifteen minutes later that she was lousy at following directions. She could get lost in Red Creek, her hometown of ten thousand people.

She stopped a few feet from the large, muscular man, swallowed several times and opened her mouth to speak. Nothing came out. Her mind emptied while he again pierced her with his arrowlike stare, his mouth pressed into a look clearly meant to intimidate.

A minute ticked into two.

Finally one corner of his mouth lifted. "Yes?"

Words slowly filtered back into her mind. "Are you Mr. Slader?"

"Just Slader."

"Can we go somewhere to talk?" She glanced around, trying her best not to let her distaste show in her expression and voice. She was afraid she hadn't succeeded, especially if the curl of his lips was any indication.

"Pull up a chair."

"Do you have an office where it's—" again she looked around "—where it's quieter?"

He chuckled. "There's no point in wasting good money on a place I'd rarely frequent. Whatever you have to say can be said here."

His grammatically correct English should have reassured her. It didn't. An education didn't guarantee he was a gentleman. "Then, can we talk over there?" she asked, aware that the man on the other side of her openly listened to every word they exchanged. She waved her hand toward a vacant table at the back of the bar that offered a bit of privacy. She could tell by the tightening about Mr. Slader's hard mouth that he was going to refuse to move. She hurriedly added, "Please."

With a frown, he shrugged and slid from the stool, allowing her to go first.

Kate wove her way through the bar to the empty table, feeling as though she were walking farther into the den of iniquity where darkness prevailed, which in actuality was correct. The back part of the bar wasn't well lit. Only two single bulbs, no more than forty watts each, dangled from the ceiling. One fan barely stirred the hot, damp air laced with that rancid smell of sweat and uncleaned bodies pressed closely together.

Mr. Slader slipped into one of the chairs, his face hidden in the ever-present shadows. Again, a shiver rippled down her spine as she dusted off the wooden seat and eased down onto it. Out of the corner of her eye she saw him watch her every move, his mouth hiking up in a lopsided grin. She perched on the edge, the hammering of her heart like the beating of a jungle drum, its tempo quickening the longer she stayed. A bead of perspiration rolled down her face. She brushed at it.

"Lady, you have about two minutes to explain why you need to have a private word with me before I return to my spot."

Again she chewed on her bottom lip, not sure if she should pursue hiring this man even though he had come with recommendations. And yet, what choice did she have? It wasn't as though scores of guides were lined up to take the job, especially ones who spoke English. Mr. Slader was it.

She inhaled a deep, composing breath and nearly choked on the smoke-saturated air. "I need to hire you to take me—"

"No."

"No! You haven't given me a chance to explain. I need you—"

"Let's leave it at that. I'm not for hire." He scooted his chair back, the sound scraping across the wooden floor and up Kate's spine.

"Why not?" She gripped her purse in her lap, her back ramrod straight.

Slader relaxed against the hard chair and studied the woman next to him. About all she needed to complete the picture of prim and proper schoolmarm of fifty years ago were white gloves and a hat. He noticed she had her auburn hair pulled into a tight bun and she wore sensible black shoes to match her sensible black purse and a prim gray-and-white dress, meant for church, buttoned up to her neck. A dress! Here! Hundreds of miles from anyplace remotely civilized. What in the world was she doing in Brazil, in Mandras, a hole-in-the-wall, backwater river town where only losers—or people who didn't want to have anything to do with civilization—ended up?

She was waiting for him to answer. She hadn't moved a muscle other than to grip her purse tighter until her knuckles whitened. Well, she could wait until—

"Please, I need your help."

Why did she have to go and say that? He was a sucker for responding to her, but he had to make her understand she didn't belong in the Amazon. She was about as much out of place as a snowman would be. Actually, a snowman might fare better than Miss Prim and Proper. "I can't help you. You need to get on the first boat out of here and return to wherever you came from. You don't belong, or haven't you figured that out yet?"

The tightness about her mouth softened slightly and the rigid set to her shoulders sagged just a hint. The death grip on her purse lessened, too. "I can't go home until I find my brother. If you can't help me, I'll have to find someone who will."

He leaned forward, getting a whiff of perfume that smelled like the rose garden his—he shook that memory from his mind. He never walked down that path. Ever. "Lady, there is no one else."

"Then you have to help me or…" She searched for words, her perfect white teeth nibbling her bottom lip.

She wasn't very attractive, but a lively gleam flashed into her blue eyes, making them glitter, and her full lips set in a frown that looked more like a pout. "Or what?" he asked, surprised that he had bothered. In fact, why was he sitting here talking to her at all?

"I'll search on my own." She gave a slight nod as though she was proud to have come up with that ridiculous solution.

A chuckle escaped. "Then there would be two people lost."

Her eyes closed, long dark lashes against her alabaster white skin that would be burned within an hour in the hot tropical sun. Her mouth moved but no words came out. Puzzled, he leaned closer.

When she opened her eyes and saw he was only a foot away, she gasped and shot back in her chair. "What are you doing?"

"Lady, I could ask you the same thing. I thought you were saying something to me, but I couldn't hear you."

"I was praying."

Praying! He knew he should leap to his feet and get away from her as fast as his legs could carry him. "Why?" he growled instead.

"I need you to change your mind."

He tossed back his head and laughed. "And you think that's going to do it?"

She looked him straight in the eye. "Yes."

He sobered at the serious expression on her plain face. "Prayers won't help you here. This can be an unforgiving place."

"All the more reason to pray."

His head began to throb. He had to put an end to the conversation before he found himself escorting this woman through a hostile jungle and regretting every step of the way. "Well, do it somewhere else. My answer is still no." He shot to his feet, nearly tumbling his chair back in his haste to get away from the lady.

"But I need you," Slader heard her say and decided, instead of going to the counter at the bar where he was sure she would follow him, he would head home, if he could call the single room he lived in a home. If she thought this place was seedy, and clearly she did from her expression and actions earlier, she would definitely think where he spent his nights was, too. He hoped that would deter her from following him. The last thing he needed was a woman full of religion to hire him to take her into the jungle where he would be forced to listen to her for days on end and save her sorry hide—

The sound of her sensible shoes on the wooden floor cut into his thoughts. She followed him toward the bar's swinging doors and out into the heat of a late afternoon in the tropics, a hot, seemingly lazy day. He squinted against the glare, pulled his Yankee baseball cap from his back pocket and plopped it onto his head, all without breaking stride. Now he wished he'd taken a drink of the whiskey that always sat on the bar in front of him, untouched.

"Mr. Slader," the woman called out, panic in her voice. "I'm prepared to pay you well for your services."

He rolled his eyes skyward, realizing every disreputable person in this bustling metropolis must have heard her. She might as well be wearing a sign around her neck that said Easy Target. She wouldn't make it one day in the jungle, if she even lived long enough to trek into the rain forest. His steps began to slow, something akin to a conscience pricking him.

Don't do it, Slader. He stiffened his determination to put as much distance between them as possible.

As he started to take a shortcut to his room, the sudden silence behind him alerted him. He threw a glance over his shoulder just as he was about to disappear down an alleyway. Miss Prim and Proper was nowhere to be seen. Relief should have taken hold, but instead he experienced a tightening in his gut, the hairs on the nape of his neck tingling, a sure sign danger was close.

She isn't your concern. You didn't ask her to come see you.

He wanted to walk away. He should walk away.

* * *

Kate watched the distance between her and the only guide worth his salt, according to the hotel manager, lengthening. If Mr. Slader thought he could brush her off that easily, he had a rude awakening coming. Not when her twin brother's life was on the line. She had to convince him to escort her or… She wasn't going to think of the *or else*. Not yet.

A sound behind her caused her to hug her purse closer to her and hurry her pace. She had taken only two more steps before arms locked around her middle and yanked her off her feet.

TWO

Kate opened her mouth to scream, but a hand slapped down on her face to keep her silent. Twisting and kicking did little to dislodge her from the steel-like trap she found herself in.

Her captor hauled her back into the dark shadows between the bar and the building next door. Terror froze her heart until it exploded into a thunderous beat that drowned out all other sounds. The reeking scent of alcohol and body odor accosted her while her assailant's hot breath singed her neck.

A man spoke something in a guttural voice that must have been Portuguese or Spanish. She didn't have to speak the language to know his intentions. He made them very clear by the way he pawed her and tried to yank her purse from her grip.

Lord, help me!

Mr. Slader appeared before her, all six and a half feet of him blocking the alley. Was he rescuing her or helping her assailant? She remembered her first impression of him in the bar. Ruthless would have been an apt word. Terror evolved into a raging panic that threatened to shut down her body. The world spun before her eyes as sweat poured into them, stinging them.

Mr. Slader said something to the man who held her. The arms about her tightened until her breath became trapped in her lungs and she couldn't inhale properly. One dirty hand clutched her throat and squeezed as her captor muttered a response. Blackness swirled before her, her chest on fire, her lungs burning. She blinked, trying to clear the haze from her vision.

As though in slow motion, she saw Mr. Slader rush forward, growling deep in his throat as if he were an animal cornered and forced to charge. The hand about her loosened for just a second. Something inside her snapped. She brought her elbow back, jabbing it into the man's stomach. He groaned and released her.

Kate fell to the side as her rescuer locked his arms about her assailant, embracing him like a grizzly bear attacking. Scrambling out of the way, she sucked deep breaths, searing her lungs, and looked about for a weapon to use in case her rescuer lost the fight.

The cluttered alley held only trash, tossed about as if someone had turned over several garbage cans. Nothing useful. Nothing like a large rock or a blunt, heavy object. The mere thought took her by surprise. Where had that come from? She'd never harmed a human being in her life—she went out of her way to avoid even hurting an insect. But then, she'd never been accosted before, either.

Frustrated at being a spectator, she could only watch

as Mr. Slader threw the blond giant back against the wooden wall of the building. A grunt punctuated the silence. Her captor shook his head, then fixed his gaze on Mr. Slader. The man charged forward, driving her rescuer into the opposite wall. The sound of his body connecting with the wood made her cringe.

She leaped to her feet. She couldn't do nothing. She never was able to sit by and let another do what she should do. Again she scanned the littered alleyway. Her gaze fell upon a stick—no, more like a club. Quickly, before she lost her nerve, she snatched it up and swung at the giant's head. The sound of wood connecting with flesh reverberated through the alley, causing her to wince. She offered up a quick prayer that no permanent harm had befallen her assailant—just enough discomfort to allow her and Mr. Slader to escape.

Her captor crumpled to the dirt at the feet of her rescuer. She moved forward.

"What do you think you're doing?" Mr. Slader asked, gripping her upper arm and pulling her away.

"Making sure he's alive."

"Believe me, lady, he's still breathing and we don't want to be around when he wakes up." He tugged her toward the street.

"But—"

Mr. Slader rounded on her. "Move it!"

Move it! Well, I never! She had a good mind to dig her heels into the dirt and stay put. Then she glanced back at the man on the ground and saw movement. That was when she decided she'd better obey.

Mr. Slader's hand grasped hers, and he practically dragged her down the street and into another alley. She opened her mouth to ask where they were going when she noticed a large animal scurrying across the trash. It was a rat! She dug her heels in and stopped.

He peered back at her. "We need to be far away from that man when he wakes up."

Kate dangled her hand and waved it toward the rat, which paused in its rummaging through the trash. "It's a rat. The size of a cat!"

"Yeah. So?"

"So? You want me to go near it?"

"That's the only way down the alley, so yes."

Kate should have resented his patronizing tone of voice, but the beady eyes of the rat were fixed on her as though she were its next meal. She sidled toward Mr. Slader, staying close to his side, as if he were her new best friend. "After snakes, rats are my least favorite animal."

One of his brows shot up. "And you don't think you're going to see snakes if you go into the jungle?"

"Yes, I'm sure I'll see them and I'll deal with it, since I have to in order to find Zach, but—"

"Lady, that man knows me. I need to get you out of here and back to the Grande Hotel."

"How do you know where I'm staying?"

"There's only one place in Mandras that a person like you would be staying."

"A person like me?"

"Someone who doesn't belong in the jungle, in the Amazon, in Brazil, anywhere near here. Okay? Let's go." He grabbed for her hand he had released and pulled her forward at the same time the big rat charged at her.

Kate screamed, one worthy of a helpless victim in a horror movie. The rat changed direction and scurried back under a mound of trash, the rubbish's offensive odor wafting to her and threatening to overwhelm her. Mr. Slader scowled and hauled her past the pile. Holding her breath, she hurried toward the exit, gladly following Mr. Slader now.

By the time she left the alley, now ahead of him, she rushed into a small mob of people—well, at least three who had heard her scream and were checking out what had happened. That fact bolstered her faith in the human race.

But before she could express her gratitude to them, Mr. Slader whisked her away in the opposite direction from the people gathering. A few yards from the crowd, she yanked her hand away, but he grasped it harder. "Slow down. I want to thank—"

"You were about to become their entertainment for the afternoon." Mr. Slader released her and set out in the direction toward where her hotel was located—at least, where she hoped it was.

She hastened after the exasperating man who just assumed she would follow him without question— which she did when she looked over the audience that had assembled. One man's gaze actually glinted as it roved over her. Another's cold look frosted her.

The unsavory lot gathering quickened her steps. "What do you mean *their entertainment?*" she asked, hoping she was misreading the men.

"Just that. They had come to watch, not rescue. We don't get too many women like you here. Mandras isn't in any travel agent's database."

Winded, her lungs burning from the fast pace the man set, Kate placed a hand on his arm. "Please slow down."

Mr. Slader halted, his attention fixed on her hand about his arm. Then he shifted his sharp regard to her face, and she was positive the temperature in the tropics had just set a record high. Even more beads of perspiration popped out on her forehead.

Finally realizing she still touched him, she snatched her hand away, feeling the scorch of his scrutiny. "They might have been coming to help. You don't know for sure." Then she remembered the toothless grin on one man's face, that too-appreciative gleam on another's, and doubted her declaration.

He barked a laugh. "I know most of these people. Believe me, lady, no one was prepared to help you."

"You did."

His eyes widened for a few seconds before he chuckled. "True. But I'm about to rectify that mistake. After I deliver you to your hotel, you're on your own, lady."

"My name is Kate Collier, Mr. Slader."

"And my name is just Slader. There is no *mister* in front of it so stop using it." He started down the dirt street riddled with grooves and holes, rainwater filling them and disguising their depth. "Let's get going before our friend back there decides to investigate the scream. I'm sure everyone in this half of Mandras heard it. You don't want Slick to discover your where-abouts."

Even though perspiration rolled in rivers down her face and soaked the cotton material of her dress, just the mention of her assailant sent her half running after Mr.—no, just Slader. "You think he'd come after us."

"There is no *us*."

She was sure she saw him shudder when he said the word *us*. How could she possibly convince him to guide her deep into the jungle, miles up the Zingu River to where Zach had last been heard from? Well, it was obvious Mr. Slader—she wouldn't let herself think of him any other way—hadn't met a person whose faith in the Lord made it possible to do anything. She had gotten this far without any harm befalling her. Some-how, she would convince Mr. Slader to help her. She hadn't figured out how yet, but she would, with the Lord's help.

After walking at almost a jog for ten minutes, he came to a stop. His brow covered in sweat, he removed his baseball cap and ran the back of his hand across his forehead. That was when Kate noticed his white, button-down shirt with his sleeves rolled up above the elbows, drenched and clinging to his body, revealing his muscular build even more. She looked away, pulling another tissue from her purse to dab at her face, glad for the moment of rest.

When she was through, her tissue was wet and she looked around for a trash can. In Red Creek there was one on every corner in the downtown area. Of course, this wasn't exactly downtown Mandras and certainly not downtown Red Creek. She wasn't even sure Mandras had a downtown area unless someone considered it to be the dock where she'd gotten off the riverboat. That was where all the vendors hawked their wares; live animals, fish and fruit from the nearby jungle.

"Toss it on the ground like everyone else does. It'll decompose and return to nature in no time. Everything does quickly here in the Amazon."

Kate snapped her jaw closed after realizing her mouth hung open in surprise. "I do not litter. Not even in the jungle."

Mr. Slader took a step closer, then another, until only a foot separated them—way too near for her peace of mind. She was beginning to feel the other side of Mandras wasn't far enough away. And she needed him to guide her through the jungle. Oh, my!

"What do you intend to do, with your garbage, Miss Collier?"

Kate held her ground, gritting her teeth together, while her pulse rate sped, betraying her. His musky scent—not wholly unpleasant—flowed over her. "I find an appropriate trash can to dispose of my waste."

He actually blinked several times, the laugh lines at the corners of his eyes crinkling. "Are you for real?"

She straightened, sure he was insulting her. "What do you mean by that?"

"I bet you don't dare jaywalk or anything else that's against the law, for that matter."

"Contrary to what some people think—" she let her gaze trek down his length, which was a mistake. She quickly looked back up at his face, swallowing hard "—laws were not made to be broken. If everyone went around breaking the laws, chaos would rule."

"Then you have definitely come to the wrong place. Chaos rules in the jungle."

"There's order everywhere. I've read several books about the jungle—"

He held his hands up, palms facing her. "No more. There's no way a book can truly capture what the jungle is like." He pivoted. "Let's go. We've rested long enough."

Again, Mr. Slader set a quick pace and before long, Kate found herself in front of her hotel with its faded blue facade and white-painted shutters. The building was the best on the whole street, which really wasn't saying that much. She'd seen her room and didn't relish spending too much time in it. Bare and uncomfortable came to mind when she thought of it, a bit of civilization but only a bit.

He started to leave.

"Don't go." She reached to stop him and caught the air.

But he looked back at her, and she hurried toward him. "The least I can do is buy you a drink for walking me all the way back here."

One of his brows quirked. "A drink? I got the strong impression you weren't the drinking kind, that you'd never seen the inside of a bar."

"I meant tea or bottled water from the dining room," she said, fiercely trying to cling to the idea of civilization for as long as she could.

"What if I wanted something a bit stronger?"

She nibbled on her lower lip, clenching and unclenching her hands. "Water is what someone should drink in the tropics. It's the best liquid to rehydrate you. I read that alcohol really can dehydrate a person."

"What are you, a librarian?"

"I'm the secretary for my church. But I love to read and spend many hours reading good books. When I decided I would be coming to the Amazon, I devoured every book I could find. Thankfully, I'm a speed reader."

"I think I'll pass on the tea and water."

"Please join me. Give me a chance to explain the importance of seeking your help."

"I can't see you changing my mind."

"I'll pay you for your time. All you have to do is listen."

"You'll pay me just to listen to you?"

She nodded, aware of how desperate that sounded. But she was desperate. She was the last hope for her brother. He wasn't dead. She knew it and intended to prove it by finding him when everyone else had given him up for dead.

"You've got fifteen minutes." He moved toward the door that led into the lobby.

Mr. Slader walked past the entrance into the bar and sat in the corner, facing the front door, his eyes scanning back and forth. Kate took the rattan chair on the other side of the scarred table, which looked as though someone had taken a knife to it over and over. She placed her purse in her lap and clutched its leather straps.

"Zach works for a pharmaceutical company as a biochemist, heading up the research division. He loves working in the field. My brother is brilliant. Not only does he have a doctorate in biochemistry but also anthropology, with extensive knowledge of linguistic patterns among the different Indian tribes in the Amazon. This area is like a second home to him."

"Contrary to you?"

Her fingernails dug into her palms. "The rain forest holds a certain fascination for me, but reading about it satisfies my curiosity. Maybe you've heard of my brother, Dr. Zachary Collier."

His brow furrowed, his lips thinning. "I know about the search a few months back for him and his team. I was approached, but I was involved in another matter at the time. Both the Brazilian and American governments were involved, though. Your brother must have powerful friends."

"The company he works for does have some pull. But they came up empty-handed. No trace of him or the men with him. Vanished one day, just like that." She snapped her fingers. "They were supposed to call in at a certain time and missed it. No one's heard from them since."

Relaxed, Mr. Slader leaned forward, resting his elbows on his knees and lacing his hands together. "Lady, that happens down here. Some men don't want to be found. Some men just plain get lost."

"Not Zach. He knows what he's doing."

With one brow arched, Mr. Slader asked, "Contrary to you?"

"We're twins but very different in a lot of ways." She waved her hand in the air. "But we're digressing." Drawing in a large breath, she released it on a long sigh. "Zach is alive. I know it."

His brow arched even higher. "How?"

"He is *not* dead." If she said it enough times, it would have to be the truth. She'd lost everyone she'd ever cared about. She was not going to lose her twin.

"This is all interesting, but you've said nothing to change my mind." Mr. Slader started to stand.

"Have you heard of the Quentas tribe?"

Mr. Slader stopped in midmotion and sat down again, nothing relaxed about him now. "I haven't heard them mentioned in a while. No one has seen one in years. Just once about ten years ago, and the outcome of that encounter wasn't good. The expedition team that trekked through their part of the jungle disappeared and was never heard from since. People don't go there anymore."

Kate sat on the edge of her chair, glanced around to make sure no one was listening and said, "Zach made contact."

"How do you know that?"

"He e-mailed me a cryptic note the day before he disappeared. He was excited about his discovery. In fact, that was one of the reasons he had returned to that area. He heard some fascinating stories about this tribe's incredible healing powers. He wanted to investigate."

The line of Mr. Slader's jaw hardened and his eyes narrowed. "Why are you telling me this?"

"His contact was someone he felt would be a bridge between him and the Quentas. If what he believed is even half-true, it's worth the risk. The benefits to mankind could be enormous."

"And the profits, too?"

"Zach has never cared one way or another about the money. He has more than enough money to do whatever he wants. He's always used his knowledge to help others, sometimes at great risk to himself."

"How do you know I won't betray you? Take your money and leave you out in the jungle to fend for yourself?"

Kate straightened her shoulders until pain shot down her back. "I'm not a complete fool. Zach knew someone in the military—General Halston. When he disappeared, I called the general, at first to insist they continue the search. When that became impossible, he recommended you. He said you were trustworthy and knew this area of the jungle well. He said you were skilled in keeping yourself and others alive. That you knew several different Indian dialects. That you were the only one for the job. The management at this hotel agreed."

"The general didn't try to stop you from searching on your own?"

"I didn't tell him I would participate personally in the search, just that I would finance one."

"It'll be expensive."

"Like I said, Zach is wealthy. He not only works for the pharmaceutical company, he owns part of it." She bent forward, putting as much emphasis on her words as she could and still talk in a low tone. "Even if he didn't have the money, I would spend my last dime looking for him. He's all the family I have."

Mr. Slader came closer, almost nose to nose. "People go into that part of the jungle and don't come out. That's the way the Quentas tribe wants it, even if Zach had a so-called contact with them."

For a few seconds Kate wondered why she didn't smell alcohol on his breath. She remembered the drink sitting in front of him at the bar. Had she caught him before he had started drinking? She'd gotten the impression he had been there for quite a while. Yet there was a lot about Mr. Slader she didn't know—starting with what his full name was.

"I will make it," Kate said.

He pulled back, shaking his head. "How can you say that?"

"The Lord will provide a way." She placed her palm over her heart. "I know it in here."

The searing heat of his gaze lit on her hand, which was splayed across her chest—briefly before moving up to connect with hers. "You'll need more than your faith to make it, lady."

She forced a smile to her lips. "That's what I have you for."

His dark eyes grew round, almost as though a surge of panic took hold of him. "You don't have me."

"According to General Halston and the locals I talked with, you're the best. If you can't do it, then no one can. And you're an American, so I don't have to worry about a language barrier."

"Flattery doesn't work on me. Besides, what I'm afraid of is that no one can do what you ask."

A calmness descended, and Kate relaxed, beginning to see the Lord doing His work. "I didn't think you were afraid of anything. The stories General Halston told me about your bravery in the Gulf War—"

"Then I would be a fool," he cut in before she could finish her sentence. "There's a lot in the jungle to be wary of."

"I know. I've read about the snakes, the caiman, the—"

He waved her silent. "Not just the animals. Books don't even begin to tell you what dangers there are in the jungle."

"The plants? The Indians?"

"Even the outsiders. Man has tried to reap rewards like gold, gems and oil from the unforgiving rain forest. The jungle doesn't want to give them up."

"You make it sound like it's a living, breathing thing."

He cocked his head. "It is."

"Will you lead my expedition?" She swallowed to coat her suddenly dry throat, her palms sweaty about the straps of her purse. "I need you."

His intense look burned into her, and she felt as though she had been left in the sun too long.

"General Halston told me you have a few debts. I can take care of them and then some."

"Who doesn't have debts?" He shrugged, but there was nothing casual about the gesture.

"But from what I understand, some men don't wait

forever to get paid. You could use my money." She named an amount she'd pay him to lead her into the rain forest.

His brows shot upward. "I don't see how you expect to find him when two governments and his company couldn't."

"I want to leave tomorrow. He's been gone almost six weeks and the rainy season will be upon us in a month, so time is of the essence."

He laughed. "I haven't said yes. And haven't you heard of outfitting an expedition? That doesn't happen overnight, not if you want it done right. And if you don't, I'm not your man."

Her breath caught at the way he said "your man." Suddenly the enormous step she was taking gripped her like the jaws of a caiman—tight, suffocating, as it pulled its victim under the water to drown it. She surveyed the hotel lobby, the best one in town, and quaked. The realization that she was so out of her element struck her anew. "Then the day after tomorrow?"

Mr. Slader surged to his feet. "This will be no stroll in the park on a Sunday afternoon."

"I know."

"You will have to follow *my* orders. I will call all the shots."

"I know, so long as it doesn't compromise my beliefs."

"No, you don't understand. You will have to follow my orders with no questions asked. Giving me any grief is a deal breaker."

The suffocating grip about her chest tautened even

more, her earlier calmness gone. She struggled for air as though she really was drowning. She had known this wouldn't be easy. She needed the best guide available if she wanted to find her brother and make it back to civilization alive. *Lord, give me the strength to say yes. To believe this is Your will and to have faith.*

The constriction about her loosened, and she dragged in a soothing breath. Then another. "I agree."

"Then be ready tomorrow morning at seven."

She rose, feeling dwarfed by his large build. "I thought you couldn't be ready to leave tomorrow."

"I can't. But there are supplies to buy and you have the pocketbook." He eyed her black purse. "Some of the money you'll spend will be on decent clothes fit for the jungle. You wouldn't make it two feet in those ridiculous clothes and shoes."

She pulled herself up as tall as possible and didn't quite reach his shoulder. So she tilted back her head and looked him in the eye. "I know that. I've read about the type of clothes I need and I've got them."

"I'll be the judge of that. Let's go."

"Where?"

"Upstairs. Show me those clothes you bought that are suited to a jungle." He took her elbow to guide her toward the staircase.

He's going to go through my clothes? Heat suffused her cheeks. No way! She wouldn't allow it. Then she remembered that she had agreed to obey without question and wasn't sure she could keep her word. She shook off his hand and faced him.

"Do you have a problem with showing me the clothes you intend to wear?"

She opened her mouth to tell him yes, but no words came out. Zach depended on her.

He chuckled. "You didn't last very long. I'd say maybe one minute, possibly two."

"What do you mean?"

"You're challenging me."

"I haven't said a word."

"Lady, you don't have to. It's written all over your face." He turned to walk away.

"Stop. Don't go."

He shifted his weight, glancing back at her. "Be one-hundred-percent sure. If you don't follow through on your end of the bargain, I'll turn around and bring you back to Mandras so fast your head will spin."

Her teeth bit into her lower lip. She nodded. She led the way up the stairs to the second floor and down the long hallway, their footsteps on the wooden planks the only sound. After taking her key out of her purse, she had started to fit it into the lock when she noticed her door was slightly ajar. Her hand reaching forward, trembling as she snatched it back.

"I know I locked my door. I always do."

Mr. Slader shouldered her out of the way. "Stay back."

THREE

Mr. Slader eased the door open and peered into the room. The set of his jaw underscored the danger that suddenly vibrated in the air. His back stiff, he moved through the entrance. With her heart pounding a maddening pace, Kate followed, peering inside. She gasped.

Her hand shook as she gripped the door frame and leaned into it for support. Before her lay everything she'd brought with her to the Amazon tossed about the room, the clothes ripped to shreds and any items she had destroyed. What caught her eye and held her stunned was her Bible in the middle of the bed, sheets of it torn out and crumpled. She nearly collapsed at the sight.

She pushed past Mr. Slader and hurried to the bed. Scooping up the pieces, she smoothed the crushed sheets and stuck them where they belonged, the whole time aware of Mr. Slader's attention on her. Silence dominated the room, the only sounds were those she made as she righted what the intruder had done to the Lord's book.

"If they think this will keep me away, they don't

know me," she muttered, completing her task as best she could and standing to face Mr. Slader, who remained by the door. "This does not scare me." Her hands continued to tremble as she held the Bible clasped to her chest, close to her racing heart.

"It should. They mean business. Do you have any idea who *they* are?" His survey took in the chaotic mess flung about the room as though a high wind had roared through, leaving everything turned upside down and inside out.

She shook her head. "That was a figure of speech. For all I know, it could be one person, two, ten. It's got to be a simple robbery. Why would anyone be after me?"

"Because you want to find your brother?"

"Zach was a biochemist doing research, not a fortune hunter looking for some treasure."

"But you said he had a good lead to where the Quentas tribe lives. The legends surrounding these Indians grow each year. Some people, I believe, think they can turn ordinary stone into gold."

"Don't be ridiculous. That's not possible."

"But that's one of the rumors spreading. Gold fever has struck the Amazon region. What's the real reason your brother is trying to find them?"

"You *seem* like a rational man. I know you have a doctorate in archaeology. Do you really think anyone believes that tale about turning stone to gold?"

"My, you have been busy. What else do you know about me?" A new tension cloaked the room, contradicting his casually voiced question.

"Not much. Just some facts. Mostly having to do

with when you lived in the United States, and of course, when you were in the military. Nothing really recent." And for some reason, she didn't know his full name— just A. C. Slader.

One corner of his mouth curved. "Then you really don't know very much about me, do you? I've lived in the Amazon for the past five years."

"People don't usually change at the core," she said to bolster her confidence.

"I beg to differ. People often change when they have to." He came into the center of the room and picked up an article of clothing, a white cotton shirt cut into several pieces. "It looks like I'll have to take you shopping for clothes after all. Just be forewarned there are no department stores in Mandras."

Kate sank onto the bed, the springs creaking, the sound grating against already shredded nerves. A damp, moldy odor prevailed, smothering in its intensity. For a brief moment, as she took in her ruined possessions, she allowed hopelessness to take hold. Who would do this to her? Why? Was this connected to Zach's disappearance? Or, was it really the robbery she so desperately wanted it to be? The trembling in her hands quickly spread through her body. She couldn't stop herself from shaking. What had her brother gotten himself into? That was the overriding question she couldn't erase from her mind.

Mr. Slader prowled about the room, reminding her of a jaguar she'd seen once at a zoo. He picked up pieces of clothing, a smashed camera, a shattered medical kit, and tossed them into a pile in the center of the room where he had stood briefly. All Kate could do was watch, fascinated by his movements.

She hugged the Bible even tighter against herself and drew strength from its feel in her hands. Someone might have succeeded in destroying her Bible, but he could never take the words she had memorized over the years. She carried them around in her heart where they gave her solace, especially in times like this. Drawing on them now, she stiffened her resolve to continue forward with her search for her brother. He would never abandoned her and she wouldn't him.

"Do you still want to start at eight tomorrow morning?" she asked, hearing the quavering lilt to her words.

"I'll be here at seven. We'll grab something to eat, then head out." He paused in his attempt to help clean up some of the mess and stared at her. "Do you want me—" He bit back the last of his sentence, a frown slashing harsh lines into his face. "Are you going to be all right by yourself?"

Kate rose on shaky legs, squared her shoulders and looked him in the eye. Had she imagined for a few seconds a softening in his tone of voice? Taking in his fierce expression right now, she dismissed that impression. There was nothing soft about this man. "I have no choice. Yes, I'll be all right."

"We always have choices. You can leave."

"Even if I wanted to leave, I couldn't tonight, so I'm hoping whoever did this has gotten what he wanted and won't do anything else tonight."

"How about tomorrow night?"

"Is it possible to leave tomorrow afternoon?"

"No."

"Then I'll deal with it tomorrow night when it comes." *One problem at a time,* she thought. Otherwise she would feel overwhelmed and leave on the next boat out of here no matter its destination. Just thinking of what she was about to do made her quake in her practical, comfortable shoes.

"Okay," Mr. Slader said slowly, making his way around the pile of destroyed items and toward the exit. "With that in mind, our first problem will be acquiring transportation upriver." He jerked the door open. "Seven, in the lobby. We have a lot to do."

Slader stood for a moment outside her room, scanning the hallway, counting the closed doors. Ten rooms in all. Maybe there was one available for him. The second he thought that, he wanted to snatch the idea back. He was her guide, not her bodyguard.

But ten minutes later in the lobby, he palmed the key to the room next to hers. He was a light sleeper and the walls were thin. He couldn't see her agreeing to him staying with her in the same hotel room to keep her safe, so this was the next best thing. He was doing it because she was right. He needed the money. Every danger signal went off in his brain that this wasn't the way to make that money, that she would make life difficult the whole way. She reminded him of everything he had tried to escape by staying in the jungle. The only good thing was that the kind of money she was offering would get him completely out of debt. He would have to keep that in mind when he wanted to shake some common sense into her.

Late the next afternoon, Kate dragged one foot behind the other as she and Mr. Slader headed back toward the hotel after completing their "shopping spree" for all the items they would need for their trek into the jungle. The sun was rapidly descending, having sapped the last of her energy an hour ago. The clothes she wore hung off her, damp, emitting an odor she would never have allowed back in Red Creek. The few tissues she'd brought with her in her purse had been used up by midmorning. She'd had to resort to wiping her brow with the sleeve of the same dress she'd worn the day before, something a lady would never do back home. And still, sweat ran into her eyes, stinging them.

The air in the lobby was cooler due to the ceiling fans that whirred overhead. Kate stood directly under one and welcomed the hot breeze from it. Blowing hot air was better than stagnant hot air. She would never take air-conditioning for granted again.

The aroma of cooked meat and spices wafted to her, making her stomach rumble. She drew in a deep breath, savoring the images of food that came to mind— anything was better than their brief lunch at the pier, consisting of bananas, manioc cakes and palm-leaf-wrapped fish, baked over a fire not two feet from her. She hated fish, but according to Mr. Slader, she'd better get used to eating it because there might be times that was all there was to eat.

Kate looked toward the dining room. "Would you care to join me for dinner?"

He peered toward the bar next to the dining room, then at Kate. "Since we're leaving early tomorrow, we'd better enjoy what food Mandras has to offer while we can. Our supply will be limited in the jungle."

"Is that a yes?"

He nodded.

Relief, which surprised Kate, flooded her. She would chalk it up to not wanting to eat alone. She was a social person and even their limited conversation today was better than no conversation.

She sat at the table farthest from the door because Mr. Slader indicated that was where they should sit. Again he took the chair that faced the entrance into the dining room, which Kate realized was a generous term to use for the room the hotel had set up to serve meals. There were seven tables with grass-woven place mats, stained with she didn't even want to know what, and mismatched utensils wrapped in paper napkins that appeared to not have been used before. The brown plastic glasses were clean at least and the table didn't wobble like the one that morning at breakfast.

For her benefit, Mr. Slader read out loud the menu posted on a chalkboard on the wall by the door. Kate wanted to groan. More fish. The last item was a chicken dish, which she promptly jumped on, giving her order to the little man with dark hair and almond eyes who hovered near her shoulder. Mr. Slader translated into Portuguese for her. The waiter bobbed his head and grinned, several of his teeth missing.

While the waiter shuffled away, Kate took a look around at the other diners. There were five, all men. While they had been shopping she had seen few women other than Indians. She knew before she'd left the comforts of her home in Red Creek that she was going to the upper reaches of the Amazon into a part that wasn't frequently traveled, and until recently, had been home to some very hostile tribes. The last holdout was the Quentas Indians, but her brother felt he would be safe after he had made that initial contact. To him, discovering a potential wonder drug was worth what risk there was. She would put her faith in her brother that he was right, but most of all in the Lord to see him and her safely through this…adventure. She couldn't find any other word to describe what was happening to her.

Mr. Slader toyed with his plastic glass of bottled water as though he didn't know what to do with it. Kate took a sip of the lukewarm drink and wished for some ice cubes. With visions of taking the cube and running it along her brow, then down her cheeks and finally her neck, she finished off her water, deciding she would never take ice for granted again, either. The waiter left the bottle by her glass. After refilling her drink, she looked up and caught Mr. Slader studying her.

She was determined not to flinch or look away. "Do you think we have enough porters? I can afford more if you think they are needed."

"We'll have to be satisfied with the two I hired."

"Why? If we need another one or two—"

"Because," he cut in, "no one else wanted to go. The

two I hired are the only ones I could get and even they were reluctant."

"Oh." She ran her finger around the rim of the glass and noticed a small nick in the plastic where it had been dropped and some of it had chipped off. "Why not? I'm paying good money."

"And that's why we were able to get those two. Money isn't everything to some people."

"I know that."

Mr. Slader shifted in his chair, bending forward and resting his elbows on the table. "People are afraid of that part of the Amazon. Many in this area are very superstitious. Centuries of beliefs can't be changed because civilization wants to move in."

"I know there are rumors, but—"

He moved closer. "Lady, they are more than rumors. It's a fact up until twenty years ago, a couple of the tribes of this region were headhunters. Do you want me to explain the process to you?"

She shook her head, lifting her refilled glass to her lips, her hand trembling. In the marketplace at the pier, she had seen a shrunken head hanging in a booth. The image that came to mind left her cold to the bone, underscoring how different everything in the Amazon was from her way of life in Red Creek.

"So we'll have to manage with the two porters and hope there aren't too many waterfalls that have to be portaged around." He let his gaze travel over her before coming back to rest on her face. "It doesn't look like you've spent much time at a gym back home."

"I walk every other day for several miles, and when

I was waiting for my visa to come through, I increased it an extra mile every day."

"I'm impressed."

His flat tone and sardonic look certainly belied his words. She ground her teeth. "I know that isn't enough. But I won't hold you back."

His brows shot up, doubt clearly in his expression now.

"I'm tougher than I look," Kate said in answer to his silent question. She would make it and she wouldn't hold the expedition back because she had to find her brother. Sheer determination had to count for something. That, and faith in the Lord would make up for her lack of physical strength.

After the waiter put their plates in front of them, Slader said as he picked up his fork, "We'll discuss how fit you are after you've trekked through the jungle for a day."

"We'll do just that."

Kate clasped her own fork and cut into the overdone piece of chicken. The vegetables on her plate didn't look familiar, but there was no way she would ask Mr. Slader what she was eating. She'd check them out in the book she'd brought concerning the plants and animals of the region. It was still readable, even if some of the pages were torn.

As she took her first bite, from beneath lowered eyelids, she watched Mr. Slader eat. She wasn't sure how he managed to cut his fish and still observe his surroundings. But she didn't think anyone in the room and the lobby beyond had escaped his notice. That fact reassured her more than General Halston's and the locals' recommendations. She might not like Mr. Slader, but she'd picked the right man for the job, especially after the trouble the evening before.

After forcing half of her chicken and most of the vegetables down her throat, she sat back, wiping her mouth with her paper napkin. She preferred eating five small meals a day rather than several large ones. She couldn't stuff another bite into her.

"You'd better finish your dinner. Chicken won't be on the menu for a while unless we're lucky enough to find a turtle to eat. It's similar in taste to chicken."

"A turtle! I couldn't eat a turtle. I had one as a pet once."

"Listen, lady, when you're out in the jungle, you can't be choosy about where your next meal comes from."

"Please call me Kate." *Lady* made her sound so—old. And suddenly, she didn't want to feel all thirty-eight years. She already didn't move as fast as she once had and her eyesight was changing. Some things from a distance were fuzzier than before. She used to be able to bend over and touch her toes and the floor. Now she was lucky if she could reach her ankles. But there was no way she would share that with Mr. Slader. They didn't have time to wait until she was in shape to go into the jungle in search of her brother. That might never happen, knowing her track record for dieting and exercising.

Mr. Slader sighed. "Kate, you can't pass up an opportunity for a full meal. In the rain forest, it probably won't happen often."

"But we're taking food with us." She thought about the large backpack she would have to carry loaded with supplies, mostly food items, a few toiletries, a change of clothes and a hammock, and wished she had lifted weights in addition to walking.

"I don't know how long we'll be gone. There are four of us and the food supply is only meant to supplement what I hope to find in the jungle. But if you want to make good time, we won't have a lot of it to forage for food."

She bristled at his voice, overly patient as though he was explaining something simple to a dense child. She pushed the plate toward him. "Then by all means, finish it off if you want. I can't eat another bite." She pronounced each word very slowly, hoping to be equally condescending.

He shrugged. "Don't say I didn't warn you." Then he took his utensil and forked the chicken.

"I promise you I won't say a word." And she wouldn't, even if she was starving. He had issued a challenge, and he would shortly realize what determination really meant. Didn't he know she drew her strength from God and could do anything she set her heart to?

When he slid her piece of meat into his mouth, Kate felt transfixed by the action. She watched him chew it, savoring it as though it was the finest cuisine.

After finishing her chicken, Mr. Slader started to toss some money onto the table to pay for the meal. He stopped, pocketed his cash, and relaxed back in his hard wooden chair, silently waiting for her.

"We'd better get to bed if we're gonna be on the river by sunrise. We'll travel when it's light. The jungle is difficult enough with the benefit of light."

"You won't get an argument out of me."

He rose, flinging down his napkin. "Good. I'm sure I'll be reminding you of those very words sometime over the next few days."

After paying the bill, Kate started for the entrance to the dining room, aware of Mr. Slader following closely behind. Goose bumps skittered across her skin, and she resisted the urge to squirm as she covered the length of the lobby. When she began to climb the stairs and he did, too, she stopped and turned toward him.

"You don't have to walk me to my room. I doubt anyone trashed it while we were at dinner."

"Probably not."

She blocked him on the stairs to the second floor. "Then I'll meet you tomorrow morning in the lobby at five."

"Fine."

She twisted around and started up the staircase again. He did, too. Glancing over her shoulder, she said, "Is this a momentary lapse in character?"

He cocked his head in question.

"Being the gentleman?"

He snorted. "Hardly. My room is next to yours."

She nearly stumbled on the last step. Gripping the bannister, she righted herself before he had a chance to reach out and touch her—that wouldn't do at all. She hurried up to the second-floor landing. "It is? Since when?" Panic laced her words.

"Last night."

"Why?"

He shifted his weight from one foot to the other, his intense gaze sliding away. "Just protecting my source of income."

Source of income? She pointed to herself. "You mean me?"

"Yes."

She wasn't sure if she should be insulted, exasperated or flattered by his remark. "I can take care—"

He took a step nearer. She took a step back, then another until she came up against the hallway wall.

"I'm sure you can, lady." Sarcasm dripped from his words.

But that wasn't what caught her full attention. His nearness and his musky scent held her transfixed.

"That is, if you were in Red Creek. But you aren't—lady. Has it occurred to you someone might not want you to go looking for your brother? What if Slick was paid to kidnap you yesterday? Or worse, to kill you? I tried to find him last night and couldn't. He's disappeared. What if the trashing of your room wasn't just a simple robbery attempt? I don't like co-incidences. Why would someone not want your brother found?"

She shook her head, words gone from her mind as though she'd lost the ability to string them together. Shocked, not so much from what he had said as from his continued nearness, all she could focus on was the brightness in his dark eyes, the white scar on his cheek, thin and in stark contrast to his tanned skin, the fullness of his mouth, firmed in a frown at the moment and directed totally at her.

"I don't know why," Kate whispered.

He stepped back, giving her some breathing space. "Since I didn't think you would want to share a room, I did the next best thing. I got the one next to you and paid to have the person in that room moved to another one. It will be on your bill in the end."

For a fleeting moment, she'd been touched that he'd cared about her safety—that was until his last sentence. Long ago, she'd given up the illusion that a man could care about her. She shoved past Mr. Slader and headed toward her door. "Of course." Fumbling with her key, she dropped it and it clanged to the wooden floor.

He picked it up and leaned around her to open her door, peering inside. "Just holler if you get into trouble. I'm only a room away."

"I'll remember that when I'm fighting off the hordes of bad guys after me." She started to close her door.

He stuck his foot forward and stopped it from shutting. "You'd better take what I said seriously. There's more going on here."

"I didn't hire you to be my bodyguard but my guide. And I'm taking this very seriously. My brother's life is at stake."

"Not just your brother's, but yours, as well."

She notched her chin up an inch. "And yours, too."

He grinned, but the dark orbs of his eyes remained cold. "Yes, and mine, too." He pulled the door shut for her and she didn't hear his footsteps move away until she'd locked it.

She collapsed back against the wooden slab that was her measly protection against the outside world, not a very good one, since she had been robbed. One hand gripped the knob as though that action would keep her upright.

What had she gotten herself into? She'd been so tired yesterday evening that beyond straightening the room and eating dinner, she'd gone right to bed and hadn't thought of anything. She didn't believe in coincidences, either. Mr. Slader was right, though she wished he wasn't. Who could possibly want to stop her from looking for her brother? Had he stumbled onto something worth killing for? The direction of her thoughts caused her to tremble. She hugged her arms to herself and pushed away from the door. When she found her brother, they would work together to discover if someone wanted to stop him or laugh over Mr. Slader's silly assumption.

With her resolve firmly in place, Kate gathered her soap, toothbrush and bottled water so she could head to the bathroom at the end of the hall, one shared by everyone on the floor. Thankfully, it was unoccupied, so she didn't have to wait in the hall. She quickly washed up, trying very hard not to notice the rust stains in the sink or shower or the less-than-clean state of the room. But when a *very* large roach ran across the floor, she jumped, covering her mouth to keep her scream inside. It scurried behind the toilet, prompting Kate to rush through brushing her teeth then snatching up her grooming items.

She started for the door when someone pounded on

it. She froze, looking around as though she needed to hide.

"Hurry up in there. You have people waiting."

Mr. Slader's voice boomed, followed by another pounding. Relief drooped her shoulders, and she opened the door to find him standing on the other side with his arms crossed and a disgruntled look on his face.

"I should have known it was you taking all this time," he muttered, pushing past her.

She should have let his comment go, but for some reason she couldn't. "Fifteen minutes isn't considered a long time where I come from."

"Everything is different here."

"So you say." She turned to go back to her room.

His hand on her arm halted her progress. "I hope you enjoyed this bit of civilization—" he jerked his thumb to indicate the bathroom "—because starting tomorrow, it gets a whole lot worse."

She yanked her arm from his grasp, gave him her best glare and stalked away. She felt his focus on her the whole way to her room and chalked it up to him protecting his meal ticket, not to anything that meant he cared if she lived or died.

Inside her room, she undressed and pulled back her covers to check for unwanted guests in her bed, still remembering that large roach in the bathroom. Knowing five in the morning would be there before she realized it, she slipped between the gray-tinged sheets then, because it was so muggy, tossed the covers off her.

Lying in the bed that creaked with each movement,

the room thrown into shadows from the light streaming in through the dingy curtains that didn't completely cover the window, she watched the ceiling fan go around and around, stirring the hot air and only giving off marginal relief. It, too, creaked with each rotation, a rhythmic sound that became a lure that drowned out the other sounds of the night—loud music, boisterous laughter and an occasional shout. Slowly her brain shut down, and her eyelids grew heavy until the darkness came.

A thump brought Kate fully awake. With a start she bolted straight up in bed. Fear clawed at her chest as she scanned her room for an intruder. A muffled sound, as though someone was saying no over and over came to her, then a crash—like a table being knocked over.

Kate scrambled from her bed, fumbling for something to throw over the large T-shirt she was using for a nightgown. She grabbed for her yellow satin robe that had been torn in several places but was still wearable. The sounds were coming from Mr. Slader's room. The thought that he was in trouble prodded her forward without really thinking through what she was doing.

FOUR

As Kate headed toward her door, she grabbed up the machete that she had insisted she have so she could do her share of the work, then charged out into the hallway, half-expecting to find people gathered to see what had caused the loud racket. The corridor was empty. She hurried to Mr. Slader's door and tested it to see if it had been unlocked. It didn't budge, and yet she could hear sounds like groans coming from inside. Was he wrestling with someone or hurt?

Unsure what to do next, she peered around her, then began banging on the door. If she couldn't get inside to help him, maybe at least she could scare his intruder away. That thought brought her up short. Where would the intruder flee to? The hallway where she was?

Her bravery wavering, she backed up, clutching the machete in both hands and raising it up in front of her. She braced her feet apart, every muscle in her body locked as she had seen someone in a movie do once.

The sounds stopped. But the thundering in her ears

vied with the silence that now ruled. She hadn't thought it was possible to tense any more, but she did.

The door flew open.

Her eyes grew round.

His hands fisted, Mr. Slader stood in the doorway, shirtless, with a scowl on his face, his long black hair loose and tousled about his wide shoulders. Then he saw her, threw back his head and laughed. "What do you think you're going to do with that?" He pointed at the machete, still held up before her.

"I was—I was—" She cleared the thickness in her throat and brought the weapon to her side, her attention still riveted to his chest heaving with his mirth. "I was going to save you."

His laughter increased.

She glanced about to see if they had gathered a crowd now that *he* was making such a racket with his merriment. Thankfully the hallway remained empty. The way things had been going lately, it would have been just her luck that someone would have finally decided to investigate the commotion. "I'm glad you think it's so funny. Next time I'll let the intruder get you."

He sobered some, but the amusement still shone in his dark brown eyes. "I appreciate you coming to my rescue, but as you can see, there was no intruder."

"I heard noises, groans coming from your room, something crashing to the floor. I thought—"

He covered the few feet to her, his movement cutting off her flow of words, and pried the weapon from her hands. She dug her teeth into her bottom lip. He was so close she could almost touch him… But she wouldn't think about that.

"I must have been dreaming." He shrugged. "That's all. No big deal."

"But—"

He turned her toward her room and gently pushed her forward. "You need your sleep. It's gonna be a long day tomorrow."

Before going inside, she reached to take back her machete.

He pulled it away from her grasp. "I think I'd better keep this. I wouldn't want you to hurt yourself before we even leave."

She frowned. "Protecting your investment?"

Hard eyes without an ounce of humor in them bored into her. "Right. I'm glad we understand each other."

She straightened, squaring her shoulders and tilting up her chin. "Mr. Slader, we will never understand each other."

"Good night, *lady*."

As she closed her door, she realized any easing of the tension between them had vanished.

Lord, I'm going to need a lot of patience to make it through the next several weeks, and You know patience isn't one of my strengths.

The sun barely peeked over the trees on the horizon and already, rivulets of perspiration streamed down Kate's face—her entire body. She glanced down at the khaki pants and white, long-sleeved cotton shirt she wore and wondered how long they would last before they were stained, dirty and smelly. Maybe an hour if she was lucky.

Kate hurried to keep up with Mr. Slader as he threaded his way through the throng at the docks along the Zingu River. Where had all these people come from? She supposed they did their trading and whatever else they needed to do before noon and the real heat set in. Mandras was really the last bit of civilization before a vast wilderness of jungle.

Three men coming out of nowhere separated her and Mr. Slader. The nearest one leered at her, and she quickened her pace to get around the group and find Mr. Slader. As she took a step to the side, the man did, too, now smiling at her in a way that made her skin crawl. He reeked of alcohol and sweat and he hadn't shaved in days. In fact, from the deep circles under his eyes, she didn't think he had slept the night before. Kate tried sidling the other way. He mirrored her movements, his smile growing. One of his buddies came up behind her, trapping her between them. Then the other companion joined them.

The men towered over her, blocking her view of her surroundings, of Mr. Slader. Where was her knight in shining armor? He was neglecting his investment—her, she thought with dread nibbling at the edges of her mind.

Adjusting the heavy blue backpack she carried, she drew up as tall as possible, which sadly wasn't very tall, and said in her toughest voice, "Excuse me. I'm late." She winced at the squeak on the end of the last word, totally wiping away the effect she wanted to present to these bullies.

The man in front of her laughed, a gleam appearing in his eyes as though he had spotted a prey and was deciding how best to dispatch it.

Just because they were at the ends of the earth didn't mean men couldn't be gentlemen! Bristling now, she thought about shoving her way through the unwelcome admirers, but she didn't dare touch one. She cringed at the thought of all the germs on their clothes, which didn't seem to have been washed in months. One of the ruffians chewed on something then spit it out—right at her feet! She shook with fear and anger. Her stomach rolled at the sight of brown juice dribbling down his chin.

"Mr. Slader," she finally decided to shout. She swallowed the word *help,* hoping he heard her cry and came without calling any more attention to herself.

One man went flying to the side. The other two turned toward the threat. Mr. Slader appeared and relief skimmed up her spine for all of a second before she realized the ruffians were bigger and meaner looking than Mr. Slader, which she hadn't thought possible. Even she knew two against one was not good odds.

Mr. Slader said something to the first man who had approached her. Kate tensed, expecting fists to fly. Instead, the man roared with laughter, glancing her way. Shaking his head, he strolled away with his two buddies.

Her jaw dropped.

Mr. Slader came up to her and tapped her under her chin to close her mouth. "This place is teeming with insects, most of them not very tasty unless you're really desperate and hungry."

She blushed, the heat of embarrassment scorching her worse than the sun's rays. "Friends, Mr. Slader?"

"As a matter of fact, yes."

"Do all your friends accost women when they meet them?"

"You have to admit, it's rare to have a woman like you here in Mandras."

"A woman like me?" The second the question was out of her mouth she wished she could take it back. She already knew his opinion of the type of woman she was.

He leaned close, only a few inches away, and inhaled a deep breath. "One who smells of roses with skin so white it's a shame it'll be blistered from the sun in less than a day."

"I've brought sunscreen with fifty SPF, which, thankfully, wasn't ruined by the intruder the other night. Perhaps in these backwaters you haven't heard of sunscreen."

She stepped around him, to head for their boat and put an end to the conversation. But with the crowd and all the different vessels docked at the pier, she didn't know which one was hers. She had to stop and wait for Mr. Slader. *Patience, Kate.*

He ambled by her, winked, and made his way toward a craft at the far end of the floating dock. "Where's your truckload of sunscreen? Because, lady, that's what you're gonna need with that fair skin of yours."

She thought about her three-bottle supply that she'd tried to cram into her blue backpack. She had finally sacrificed a third set of clothing in order to bring them along on the trip. "I did the calculations. Three bottles should last me a month."

He chuckled, tossing her a glance over his shoulder. "Have you calculated in all the sweating you'll do? You'll have to reapply about once an hour."

"Well?" She frowned. Had she? Not really. "I'll worry about that when I run out. Besides, I read the rain forest is often dark with little sun."

"True, but our first couple of days will be on the river. All sun. And as you can see," he waved his hand toward the ten foot boat, open with no cover, "there isn't a lot of shade for you to hide under."

She stiffened. "I don't hide."

"I'll remember that the first time you see a snake."

Lord, I know there are a lot of snakes in the jungle. Please protect me from them and help me with my patience. Mr. Slader has already tested it several times and we haven't even left the pier.

Bolstered by her faith, she lifted her chin and walked past Mr. Slader. "I'll be fine. Don't worry about me. Worry about yourself."

"Myself? I know I'm gonna regret asking why."

"The Lord is with me. Is He with you?"

"Lady, *He* abandoned me a long time ago." A scowl accompanied his words.

"I beg to differ. God never abandons someone. You abandoned Him."

With as much dignity as she could muster in one-hundred-percent humidity and heat nearing eighty, she shrugged off her backpack, gripped a post and lowered herself into their craft, a large canoe that would accommodate four people and their supplies—barely. The boat rocked, and she quickly clasped the edge of the pier.

"Please hand me my pack, Mr. Slader."

When she said the word *mister,* his brows slashed downward and his mouth thinned into a hard line.

Before she had a chance to sit, he tossed her backpack at her. Her arms automatically came up to trap it against her chest, but its twenty-pound weight threw her off balance, the air whooshing from her lungs. She teetered, her hands clutching the pack so she couldn't catch herself. The brown water loomed before her as she tilted sideways.

A strong grasp locked about one arm and steadied her. For the few seconds Mr. Slader touched her, the brand of his fingers wiped the sounds and smells of her surroundings from her mind. When he released her, she sank down onto the bench, her whole body quavering. She wanted to attribute her reaction to her near dunking in the dirty brown river, but she couldn't.

She didn't dare look at him. She didn't want to see his smirk, or the "I told you so" look in his eyes. Instead, she busied herself securing her backpack next to her while he and the two porters loaded the rest of what they were going to take.

Digging into her pack, Kate withdrew a bottle of sunscreen and a white hat with a wide brim, the only shade she would have on the long journey. She plopped the hat onto her head and slathered the lotion on every exposed part of her body. When she finished, she put the bottle back in her bag and pulled out a handker-chief, then zipped up the backpack.

She was ready to go. With a sigh she folded her hands in her lap, clutching the cloth, and looked up. The amused expression in Mr. Slader's eyes pushed her anger button.

"I suppose you're all set now?" he asked, position-ing himself in front of her on a bench with one porter at the back and the other at the front.

"Yes, as a matter of fact, I am."

Grasping a paddle, Mr. Slader said something to the Indian porters, who each untied the large canoe from the dock and pushed off. The craft headed out into the middle of the river. Kate glanced back at the last bit of civilization she would see for a while. A man emerged from a group of men, his focus trained on her. Tingles of fear shimmied down her when she recog-nized him—Slick! And he was way too close for her peace of mind. Even from a distance she could feel the waves of animosity coming off him, all directed at her.

She quickly twisted forward and was greeted with Mr. Slader's broad back, his muscles rippling beneath the white cotton of his shirt as he stroked the water with his paddle. While she wasn't in top physical shape, it was evident he was. This was the view she would have to endure the whole trip on the river. A groan escaped her lips.

Slader peered over his shoulder. "Already having second thoughts?"

"No." She sat up as straight as possible on the bench. "Did you see Slick back at the dock looking at us?"

He nodded and resumed his position, facing forward.

Of course, Mr. Slader had seen Slick. He was aware of everything going on around him. That thought comforted her as she settled in for the long trip.

She dabbed at her face and neck with her handkerchief and stared at the green line of foliage along the riverbank, in stark contrast to the milky brown of the water and the whitish blue of the sky. A bright-colored macaw perched in the upper branch of an unfamiliar tree. The bird's red and yellow markings drew her attention. It lifted off and took flight, its squawking heard above all the other sounds. Then she saw a black monkey with a long tail and long arms swing from one limb to another, its movement graceful. There was beauty here, Kate thought, deciding it might not be so bad after all, especially if she could ignore Mr. Slader as much as possible and look upon this as an adventure she could tell everyone when she got back to Red Creek.

Thank you, dear Heavenly Father, for making this all possible. With Your guidance I will find my brother and bring him home.

Removing her pieced-together Bible from her backpack, she opened it to the beginning of the book of Acts and began to read to help pass the time. If she was lucky, she would have a lot of time to study the Lord's word while on this adventure—a bonus she hadn't thought about before they'd set off.

Kate had read through a third of the book of Acts when Mr. Slader turned and handed her a paddle. "What's this for?" she said.

"It helps move the boat from one point to another, and because the current is strong here, we need everyone to help and that includes you, *lady*."

His emphasis on the word *lady,* accompanied by a scowl, scattered any calm she'd gathered while reading her Bible. Gripping the book, she unzipped her backpack and carefully tucked it away to read later.

"Remember when we were buying the supplies, you bought your own machete. You said you would do everything I did, that you would carry your own weight. Well, I'm calling you on it." Mr. Slader turned back to paddling.

The sound of his slicing through the water competed with the noises from the jungle on both sides of Kate—the different calls of birds, the chirping of insects. While reading she'd managed to block the sounds from her mind, but now she heard above the birds and insects a distant rumble. "What's that?"

"The waterfall up ahead."

Clasping the paddle, Kate dipped it into the brownish murk floating by them. The force of the current almost snatched it from her grasp. She tightened her hold and put all her strength behind it, which she was discovering wasn't much. "Waterfall? Are there many on this river?"

"A few."

The porter in front, named Pedro, said something to Mr. Slader. The other behind Kate, called Miguel, made a comment, too. Mr. Slader chuckled.

"Why do I get the feeling I am being discussed?" Kate strengthened her hold on the paddle, the muscles in her arms quivering from her efforts. Now more than ever, she regretted her inability to pick up foreign languages fast.

"Because you are. Pedro wondered how long you would last paddling and Miguel said, from the looks of your grip, not long."

"What's wrong with my grip?"

"Don't fight the water. Go with the flow as much as possible."

"But we're going upstream. That's kind of hard to do, especially right now."

"Still, you're wasting a lot of energy gripping the paddle too tightly. Ease up."

"But what if I lose it?"

"Then you can dive in and get it."

The humor in his voice irked her, especially since she'd only recently learned to swim. She would somehow manage to paddle *and* retain her hold for as long as needed. She'd put a positive spin on this. She'd think of all the pounds she would lose on this trip. She'd been wanting to go on a diet before the holidays because she knew she would eat a lot more between Thanksgiving and Christmas, so this would work out great. There! She felt so much better.

The euphoria lasted ten measly minutes. That was when Kate barely managed to lift the paddle out of the water, let alone paddle. With a shallow gasp she pulled it into the boat and laid it across her lap.

Slader glanced back at her.

"I'm not quitting, just resting for a few minutes," she said.

"We're nearly to the waterfall so wait until we go around it, then you can pick up paddling again. The current is strong in this part of the river."

She heard the amusement in his voice and almost took up her paddle for something far worse—something a good Christian shouldn't even consider. *I'm trying to do the right thing, but he isn't making it easy. I need that dose of patience—and fast, Lord.*

The roar of the waterfall completely obliterated the other sounds of the jungle as they neared it. The water became rougher and for once she saw the wisdom in doing as Mr. Slader said. Watching him struggle to paddle underscored how difficult it really was, because she had to acknowledge that the man was in good physical condition. He had been laboring for two hours and hadn't taken a break once. The only indication the heat was even bothering him was that his white cotton shirt was soaked across his broad back, which only emphasized his muscular shoulders and upper torso.

Kate found her clothes totally drenched with her perspiration. She might as well go into the river as wet as she was. But then she remembered all the animals that lurked beneath the water's surface and she shuddered.

Pedro shouted something, pointing at a spot in front of the canoe.

Mr. Slader immediately paddled hard to the left. With hers in her hand, Kate lifted herself up a few inches to see what was the problem. Her actions sent the craft rocking and the churning water lifted and dropped the canoe. Her gaze glued to several massive tree trunks in the river, she became paralyzed for a few seconds.

But doing nothing was an even bigger mistake. The sudden change of course coupled with the rough water threw her balance off. She started to fall forward toward Mr. Slader. Quickly, she tried to catch herself, forgetting that she grasped the paddle. It dropped into the water. She lurched for it, her fingers almost clasping onto it. But with her body too far over the edge of the canoe, Kate tumbled into the river, plunging headfirst into its warm, murky depths. She opened her mouth to scream and swallowed a mouthful of the dirty water.

FIVE

Slader heard the splash behind him and he cursed. Even before Miguel said anything, Slader knew that Kate had managed to go overboard. Now he would have to get wet to rescue her. And it wasn't even noon yet.

Shouting a few orders to Pedro and Miguel, he threw his paddle down onto the bottom of the canoe then slipped his tennis shoes and ball cap off while twisting about to see where Kate was. When he didn't see her emerge, worry began to knot his stomach muscles.

He dove into the river where he thought she had gone under, barely missing one of the tree trunks that floated by. Searching the cloudy water, he couldn't see or feel her. He shot up to the surface to look around, hoping that Kate had managed to come up.

The water swirled about Kate. With a hard kick she tried to swim upward.

Something snagged her shirt. She couldn't tell what

it was. She couldn't see past a few inches in front of her. She tugged on her shirt in an attempt to free herself. It wouldn't budge!

Panic seized her as tightly as whatever had hold of her. Her lungs burned. Water roared in her ears. Yanking again, she clasped the cotton material where it was caught and tried to rip it loose. She couldn't!

Trapped in a world of dark, muddy water, its taste making her stomach roil, Kate fought not to surrender to the black hole waiting to swallow her. *Lord, I'm in Your hands.*

For the third time after checking to see if Kate had emerged from the river's hold, Slader plunged back down into its depths, making a sweep with his arms as he searched the area. He had started back toward the surface when he felt his foot touch something soft. Even though there was little oxygen left in his lungs, he didn't dare go up for air then come back down.

Fighting the current to keep from being whisked away from the spot, he felt around for what his foot had connected with. Then when he didn't think he could hold his breath a second longer, he grasped Kate's arm. He pulled on it. She didn't move.

Going deeper, he found where she was ensnared on a submerged log. Prying with all the strength he had left and then some, he freed her and dragged her upward, his chest on fire. Fear took hold of him. Kate was limp in his grasp, not fighting him.

He broke the surface, hauling her up into the fresh air. Peering at her closed eyes, he realized he had to get her to shore and try to revive her. If he had a breath left in him, he was *not* going to bury another woman out here in the jungle.

Securing her to him, he swam toward the riverbank, tiring with each stroke. Another large log raced toward him. He increased his speed, desperate to avoid it. His limbs burned and quivered with the effort. The shore loomed before him. Ten yards. Five.

Finally, after what seemed an eternity, his feet touched the bottom and he pulled himself up, the water flowing rapidly around his waist. With his limbs still trembling, he bent and heaved Kate up into his arms and trudged toward a small opening in the sea of green flora along the bank. Every muscle in his body protested.

Dropping to his knees, depleted of all energy, he collapsed with Kate to the jungle floor. The jolt caused water to spew from her mouth, and she began to cough. Her eyes popped open. She turned to her side and continued to cough up the river.

Slader lay on the ground next to her, staring up at the ceiling of green and blue, listening to her. The remnant of his fear mingled with his weariness, and for the life of him he couldn't move an inch. Sucking in deep breaths, he replenished his oxygen-deprived lungs.

Pedro and Miguel brought the canoe to the shore and tied it to a protruding log a few feet away. They stayed in the boat because the small opening in the jungle was only big enough for him and Kate. He finally assessed his surroundings as her coughing calmed. On three sides, the rain forest hemmed them in. He knew of the many possible dangers that could be behind that wall of green. They needed to get out of there.

Shoving himself to a sitting position, Slader looked at her—nothing of the Miss Prim and Proper evident at the moment. She lay curled into a ball, her chin resting on her chest, her arms hugging herself. Her pale skin held an ashen cast to it, almost obliterating a strip of pink across the top of her cheeks and nose.

"We're going back," he said, his voice raw.

Through the pure exhaustion and pain, Kate heard Mr. Slader's words and squeezed her eyes closed for a few seconds while she gathered what strength she had left to answer him. Unfolding her body, she pushed up, her back flat against a tangle of green vines. She didn't feel tough at the moment, but she had to be in order to convince Mr. Slader to continue up the river.

"No. The only place I'm going is forward." She met his pinpoint look with all the determination she could muster.

"We haven't been gone from Mandras even three hours and already we have run into a problem, or rather, you have run into a problem. This does not bode well for the trip."

The steel in his voice drilled his decisiveness into her. She automatically backed up, but the brush stopped her.

"You could have died out there in that river. I was lucky I found you."

"But you did find me. It was God's will. I'm not

going to die until it's my time. Then nothing I do or do not do will stop it from happening."

"So with that kind of thinking, you could jump off a cliff with no second thoughts because you wouldn't die unless you were meant to?"

"I'm not stupid or suicidal."

He arched a brow. "You aren't?"

Anger boiled to the surface. "No, I am not, but I can't sit around worrying about everything. If that were the case, I wouldn't even get on a plane, or worse yet, drive my car. Have you seen the statistics on car accidents?" Her voice rose with each word in spite of the fact that her throat ached, the taste of the river still in her mouth.

He glared at her.

"Are you going to threaten turning around every time something happens to go wrong?"

His glare evolved into a frightening look that took her breath away. Her tongue shot out to lick her dry lips.

"I am committed to finding my brother no matter what. Do you have a sibling?"

His mouth hardened a bit more around the edges which she hadn't thought was possible. "Yes, a sister."

For a brief moment she wondered about Mr. Slader's childhood, family, before she replied, "Then you must understand that I won't believe Zach died until I see his dead body."

"You could wander around this jungle a long time and never find him or his dead body." Mr. Slader peered over his shoulder toward Pedro and Miguel, then back at her. "Okay, we'll go forward for the time being. Any more foolhardy tricks like the last one and you won't be able to talk me out of returning. And we will be back in Mandras when the rainy season starts. I don't have a long time to wander around this jungle. One month, lady. That's as long as you'll have my services."

"Oh, then you have some other pressing business to attend to?" she asked to keep from thinking she didn't want to be stuck with him more than a week—let alone a whole month—thirty *long* days.

He grumbled something under his breath and rose, turning his back on her to speak to the two porters.

Kate attempted to stand and fell back on her bottom, her legs so weak they refused to support her. She wouldn't ask Mr. Slader for help if he were the last man standing. She scanned her surroundings, every shade of green represented, and found a limb above her head to the right that appeared sturdy. Grasping it, she used it to yank herself to her feet. Halfway up she came eye to eye with two black, beady ones. A tongue flicked out and she screamed.

Mr. Slader spun around.

Kate jumped back against him, and if he hadn't held her by her upper arms, they would have both ended up in the river again.

She stared at the spot where she had seen those two beady eyes and flicking tongue and pointed her finger. "A snake!"

Releasing his hold and coming forward, Slader examined the area she indicated. "Which you have obviously scared away with your scream."

Glancing at him, she saw him stick his finger in his ear. "Good."

"Lady, I don't know if anyone has told you, but you have a very effective voice."

"I sing in the choir at my church. Soprano."

"That must explain the high pitch. Next time, however, warn me first so I can step back a few feet and cover my ears."

Pedro made a comment from the canoe, and Slader responded to him, then laughed. She really was going to have to learn Portuguese. Or, maybe ignorance was truly bliss.

"We need to get going. We won't stop until we have to portage around the falls. We have about a half a mile to go before we reach the waterfall."

"It sounds like it's just around the bend."

As she passed him to step into the canoe—very carefully—he said, "It's very big."

Not too much later, Kate discovered for herself just how big.

Mr. Slader used hand signals to indicate what to do, because of the noise from the water crashing down sixty feet into the river ahead, a fine mist shrouding the surrounding jungle. She craned her neck to stare at the top of the cliff. They had to climb up the side of the falls with the ten-foot-long canoe and their supplies. The enormity of the task hit her like the water tumbling down and striking the river ahead.

Despite the sun beating down relentlessly, her clothes were still damp, making her shiver. The worst part of her topple into the river earlier was that she'd

lost her one and only hat. Even though she had reapplied the sunscreen with a generous coating on her
now-exposed face, her worry intensified that Mr.
Slader was right—three bottles wouldn't be nearly
enough.

Pedro hopped off onto some boulders, gripping the
front of the canoe to hold it in place while Mr. Slader
crawled forward. The craft bounced about on the
churning water. The porter struggled to keep the boat
anchored.

After Mr. Slader made it to the rocks and helped
Pedro, he motioned for her to make her way to him.
She blocked the rocking motion and the roiling water
from her mind and instead concentrated on staying
low in the canoe and creeping forward one inch at a
time. Going over in this part of the river could prove
fatal with the rushing water and large boulders all
about, especially when she'd only had a handful of
swimming lessons, and those had been only two weeks
ago. When she neared him, Mr. Slader grasped her arm
and assisted her to the rocks.

Close to her ear, he said, "Make your way over
there." He pointed behind him where there was a small
opening in the dense brush.

She nodded and began picking her way toward the
area indicated. On the wet, slick rocks, one foot went
out from under her. She fell, scraping her shin, the
cotton material of her pants ripping. Glimpsing Mr.
Slader, she was glad he hadn't seen her mishap. Carefully, she stood again and continued forward, all her attention focused on where she placed her next step.

She still had one boulder to go when Pedro and Miguel, barefoot, passed her, carrying the canoe over their heads. She sensed Mr. Slader right behind her. Even though she couldn't hear his approach, she felt his stare. She threw him a look over her shoulder, glad the waterfall's roar kept them from carrying on any kind of conversation. Impatience stamped his features. She wasn't going to hurry the last few steps. Already her shin hurt from her last encounter with the rocks.

When she ascended to firm, level ground, she sent up a silent prayer of thanks to God for getting her through the past few hours relatively unharmed. Mr. Slader took her arm and prodded her forward. *No rest for the weary,* she thought, but wouldn't say a thing to him.

He led them up the side of the waterfall, carrying the extra supplies while Pedro and Miguel transported the canoe. Kate felt guilty for only managing her twenty-pound backpack until she was a third of the way up the falls and could barely put one foot in front of her. And they weren't even at the steepest part of the climb!

Gritting her teeth, she trudged behind Mr. Slader with a pack slung over each arm and the paddles in his hands. Pain from the tense set of her jaw shot down her neck as she marveled at the physical shape the man was in. She'd assumed he usually sat in the Blue Dolphin Bar most of the day and night, downing one drink after another. So how did he do it?

Her wet clothes, coupled with her hiking boots, felt as though they added an extra fifteen pounds. Yet she was determined to do this if it was the last thing she did.

Slader paused and turned to check on them. One look at her face and he frowned. "Do you need me to carry your backpack?" he shouted over the noise of the falls.

The worried way he phrased the question ruffled her feathers, and she straightened as tall as she could with the twenty-pound pack on her back and shouted, "I can handle it."

Doubt curved one corner of his mouth up and lifted both eyebrows.

Somehow she managed to raise her hand to gesture toward the path ahead. "Look, we're almost there. Worry about yourself."

With a shrug, he pivoted and started up the trail.

Pride goeth before the fall—those words taunted her each step she labored to take. *Okay, Lord, I was wrong. I should have accepted his assistance even though it would have come with a smirk and a comment that I don't belong anywhere near a jungle. He's right. I know. I should be home right now, going about my daily routine. But Zach's out there. I can't sit back and do nothing.*

As she talked to God, she forgot about the exhaustion that cleaved to every inch of her and the fact that her body ached in places she hadn't realized could ache. She began to look about her and noticed the primitive beauty that graced the rain forest. A yellow-and-green bird took flight from above her and soared across the river. Following its escape, she tripped. With quick reaction she saw the tree root in the path and caught herself before falling.

Stay focused on the trail, she told herself, realizing yet again what a novice she was when it came to the jungle; actually, to anything having to do with the outdoors. She didn't like to go camping, whereas Zach had, and had gone many times while they had been growing up. She liked her indoor bathrooms and a nice soft bed without all the insects and animals, especially the snake variety. And thinking of the comforts of civilization, she missed air-conditioning the most.

At the end of their forced march to the top of the cliff, Mr. Slader stopped at a small clearing, shrugging off the backpacks and dropping the paddles at his feet. His labored breathing and sweat-drenched clothing were the only indication that he had been bothered by the climb.

Kate, with her pack still on her back, wilted to the jungle floor. Her dry mouth and throat screamed for water while her head throbbed, the beating of her heart pulsating in her ears. It was so hot that if she had been alone, she would have removed some of her damp clothing. Then she remembered why she wore long sleeves and long pants—to protect her skin from the sun and insects.

Mr. Slader tilted back his head and drank deeply of the water in his canteen. She watched, too exhausted even to get hers out of her bag. His gaze was riveted to hers. Walking the few feet to her, he gave her his canteen. With trembling hands she latched on to it and brought it to her mouth, not caring that his had been on the same place only seconds before. She had never tasted something so delicious as this water.

Mr. Slader said something to Pedro and Miguel, who had come into the clearing. They placed the canoe in the calmer water and tied it to a tree trunk.

"We'll rest for a few minutes," Mr. Slader said to Kate, taking out his machete. "I'll be back."

He disappeared into the brush, and for a long moment Kate fought to keep her panic from erupting. What if he didn't come back? What if something got him? Zach had disappeared in the jungle. What if Mr. Slader did, too? She looked at the two porters by the canoe and remembered she couldn't speak their language, which didn't help her panicky feeling.

Closing her eyes, she bowed her head and whispered, "Lord, I can't get frightened every time something new happens. I'll live in a constant state of fright. Please help me to see the wonder and beauty in this new experience and to trust in Your guidance. In the name of Jesus Christ, Your Son, amen."

"You really thinks those prayers are gonna help you?"

Mr. Slader's voice behind her made her cringe. She looked heavenward for inspiration in dealing with the man. "Yes, I do, or I wouldn't do it. But I'm sure you wouldn't understand."

He handed her several bananas, then gave the porters some, too. "Not understand what? That you're frightened? If you weren't, I would be worried."

She finally released the straps of the pack from her shoulders. "I'm not—" She bit down hard. "Okay, I admit, I'm scared. I almost drowned, and I saw a snake in the first few hours. Both experiences I'd just as soon not repeat."

"The first sensible thing you've said." He sat across from her and peeled one of his bananas. "We can always go back at any time. Just say the word."

Kate popped a piece of the fruit into her mouth, its taste delicious. "Where did you find these?" she asked.

Knowing she would pester him with questions if he didn't respond, he explained. "Coming up the trail, I saw them nearby and knew we wouldn't always get an opportunity so close to us. A lot of the time you have to search for food."

She nodded toward the wall of trees to her side, the sound of the waterfall downriver a reminder of the difficulty in the task before her. "I thought there would be tons of food out here in the jungle. Look at all the vegetation."

"Some are edible. Some are poisonous, so don't go eating anything unless I say you can."

Kate's grip on her banana strengthened until she ended up squashing it. She looked down at it between her fingers and sighed.

"You don't like taking orders, do you?"

Patience, Kate. "No." She began eating the now softened fruit. "Do you?"

He stabbed her with his dark eyes. "No."

"Ah, so there is something we have in common."

"But in your case, you'd better learn quickly to take orders. There might not always be time for your arguments. Remember our deal."

"Mr. Slader, I haven't forgotten our deal."

He frowned and resumed eating his bananas in silence, which was fine with Kate. Talking to him brought to the surface emotions she didn't allow in Red Creek. She didn't lose her temper or shout at people back home. Her life was orderly and calm. She had a routine that suited her, and when this was all over with, she would be able to get back to it.

A flock of parrots flew overhead and landed in the tree canopy on the far side of the river. Their insistent squawking filled the air and drowned out all other sounds for a few moments. The sun began its descent toward the horizon. Slader told Pedro and Miguel to head for the sandy beach a hundred yards up ahead.

"Why are we going to shore?" Kate asked.

He made the mistake of glancing back at her. Her red face and neck prodded thoughts of his first time in the tropics. He hadn't really known how strong the sun was near the equator. But he'd learned real fast, having suffered second-degree burns. Without her hat, she was totally exposed to the sun's rays, even with the sunscreen on, and her alabaster skin was quickly turning red.

He removed his ball cap and tossed it into her lap. "Put that on."

She picked it up. "But it's sweaty."

Her huge eyes were glued to what he knew was the wet, dirty band inside the hat. "It's the tropics. Sweating is a permanent condition down here. Put the hat on, lady."

She huffed. "Why are we going to shore now? It isn't dusk yet."

Her glare drilled into his back. He didn't have to look over his shoulder to know that. He counted to ten, but with her, counting to a thousand wouldn't be enough.

"We shouldn't waste any daylight."

He blew out a frustrated breath. "Lady, when did you become the guide?"

"Well, I—I…"

Bringing his paddle out of the water, he twisted around to face her. She still clutched his ball cap in her hand. "Put the hat on now or I'll do it for you."

Her eyes grew even wider at his harsh tone. She opened her mouth to say something, but thankfully snapped it closed and gingerly placed the hat on her head.

"If you lose my hat in the river, I'll throw you overboard to go get it. Put it on! I don't have time to babysit a woman who has second-degree burns on her face from the sun. We'll go back if I have to. Lady, that's a promise."

She pushed the bill down low on her forehead. "Second-degree burns? But I've used my sunscreen."

"When was the last time?"

She checked her watch and grimaced. "Almost two hours ago." Touching her face delicately with her fingertips, she asked, "Am I red?"

"You see that tree over there." He gestured toward the shoreline where they were heading, at a red flowering jacaranda. A Jabiru stork stood guard over her large nest in its branches, a spot of white in a sea of red. "Another fifteen minutes in the sun and you'll rival it. The nearest clinic is a day back down the river."

She frowned. "You've made your point." She paused for a long moment, mumbling something he couldn't hear—no doubt, another one of her prayers, then said, "Thank you for the use of your hat. I can share my sunscreen with you."

Strangely, her offer touched a place deep in his heart, which had hardened years ago. He didn't know what to say so he turned forward and remained silent.

"Mr. Slader."

He shuddered at the word *mister*. It made him sound civilized and he knew he wasn't anymore. That part of him had died, along with all that he had cared about once.

"You didn't answer my question. Why are we stopping?"

This time he counted to twenty before answering in what he hoped was a neutral voice, "Because it will take time to set up camp and I know this place is much better for that than the next twenty miles upriver. When the sun goes down, it goes down fast. So, is it all right with you if we stop for the night?" He really hadn't intended to throw in that last question, but he couldn't help himself. He liked ruffling her feathers. He almost felt alive when they locked horns, so to speak.

"Yes, I guess this will be okay," she answered as though she were an expert on the Amazon and the river they were traveling.

When they landed on the sandy beach, Pedro

brought the canoe up on land. Kate found some shade and put her backpack down, again pressing her fingertips to her face as though testing it for redness even though she couldn't see it. It was nice to see he had finally gotten her attention concerning wearing his hat.

He ran his hand through his hair, which felt strange since he was so used to wearing his Yankee ball cap. It had been through a lot with him. It was his last link to home, to the life he had once led and left behind.

After they set up camp, which mainly consisted of stringing up their hammocks and building a fire, Pedro began fishing. Another flock of birds flew up into the sky down the river, as though they had been frightened. Miguel made a comment to Slader about the unusual activity, the third such comment in the past hour.

He observed the flight of birds, not one species but many. The hairs on the nape of his neck rose. He didn't like the feeling he was getting in his gut. Someone was following them.

SIX

The sun appeared as though it were a large yellow ball hovering right above a green carpet to the west. Mr. Slader returned from a trek into the jungle, having been gone for ninety interminable minutes. Kate knew this because she had been pacing the beach for the past fifteen of those minutes wondering where the man was. When she saw him, she expected his arms to be full of food—what else could he be doing? Instead, he carried one cluster of palm nuts.

Trying to ignore the rumbling in her stomach, she hurried over to him. "Miguel went off in the other direction. Maybe he'll have better luck finding something to eat." She took the nuts, trying not to think of how hungry she was. If this was all he could find in the jungle after being gone for so long, what was going to happen when they ran out of the food they had brought? Suddenly she wished she were stronger and could carry more than the twenty pounds.

Mr. Slader didn't say anything and his silence alerted Kate. Something wasn't right. She stooped in the sand by the fire, preparing the palm nuts so they could eat them. "What aren't you telling me?"

One of his eyebrows shot upward. "Very perceptive."

She waited for him to tell her. He didn't. "I'm paying you to guide me, not protect me from the truth."

He jabbed his machete into the sand, its hilt facing upward. As he checked his shotgun, making sure it was loaded, alarm bells blared loud in Kate's mind. She curled her hands in the sand by her legs and waited for him to tell her what was really going on.

Finally he said, "We're being followed. I went back to see who it was."

"And?"

"Slick is one of the party. There are three others, all lowlifes who work for the highest bidder," he answered, calmly stuffing shotgun shells into his pockets. "And Slick doesn't have the kind of money to hire them. So, who does? And more importantly, why?"

Frustration and fear churned in Kate's stomach. "I don't know! Believe me, if I did, you would be the first I would tell."

"I hope so, because I'm putting my life on the line right along with yours." He placed his shotgun in easy reach.

His sentence brought home to her how much danger they were in. She wished she knew who was after her and why, then maybe she could do something about it. But she didn't know even where to begin formulating a list of suspects. She needed Zach. It had to revolve around her brother somehow. "What are you going to do about those men following us?"

"Nothing. It'll be completely dark soon. Too dangerous for us to travel on this river, but that also means it's too dangerous for them, too."

"How about over land? If you could get to them in forty-five minutes, they can get to us."

"True. But in the dark it isn't easy to travel in the jungle. Besides, I knew where they were. I don't think they're sure where we are."

"What about tomorrow?"

"Going back to Mandras now doesn't seem an option even if we wanted to. We'll continue upriver for a while longer, then cut through the jungle. If we cover our tracks, they may not realize what we're doing."

Kate shivered even though the air was hot and she continued to perspire profusely. She peered off across the river and noticed the streaks of orange and red in the darkening sky. Now that it was dusk, the mosquitos and tiny fly population increased on their small, sandy beach, swarming about her face and any exposed skin. She quickly reapplied the insect repellant she'd brought, which offered only marginal relief.

Mr. Slader added a few more logs to the fire, several wet ones, causing smoke to billow upward. "This should help some with the insects."

"Won't the fire give our location away?"

"It's a risk I'm willing to take. As I said, it wouldn't be safe traveling overland or by this river in the dark. Slick isn't smart, but he isn't a fool, either."

Total darkness fell quickly as though someone had

pulled down a shade, shutting out all light. Pedro waded to shore with his catch, his smile broad. Miguel returned from the forest with several mangoes and coconuts. Mr. Slader set about preparing their meal, offering Kate the fire-roasted fish and slices of fruit with the palm nuts.

She stared at her plate, her stomach protesting its hunger. "What kind of fish is this?"

"A piranha."

"As in razor-sharp teeth?"

"Very tasty—the flesh that is, not the teeth."

Even with the insect repellant on, mosquitoes landed on her. She slapped at her neck while she continued to glare at the piece of fish. She knew she needed to eat it even though the smell and taste repulsed her.

"I doubt I'll run into a chicken anytime soon," Mr. Slader said. "And you made it clear how you felt about turtle meat, a good source of protein in the jungle, I might add."

After giving thanks to the Lord for the food, Kate consumed everything but the fish, then after studying it for a few minutes as though that would make it change into the chicken she so desired, she dug into the piranha, determined to down it to keep up her strength. They had men following them. She had to.

She choked on the first couple of bites, then with swigs from the treated water in her canteen, she managed to finish everything. Proud, she presented her empty plate to Mr. Slader.

He nodded toward the river twenty feet away. "You might want to wash it."

"In there?" She pointed to what she knew was muddy water even though she couldn't see it in the dark.

"Use the sand as soap. I'll show you." He rose and walked toward the river.

As she followed him, more insects landed on her, and she felt some bites even through her clothing. At the river's edge, she did as Mr. Slader did, dipping her plate into the water, then her hand into the sand at her feet. Rubbing it into the metal, she scrubbed the tin plate clean, then washed off the sand. Everything she had learned in home economics class had been tossed out as though civilization no longer existed, she thought as she trudged back to their makeshift camp, glad for its fire, which offered light in the pitch-black night and some protection from the bugs that feasted on her.

Back in the smoke-filled air, Mr. Slader fed the fire with more damp logs. He spoke to Miguel and Pedro, who quickly finished eating, then climbed into their hammocks and pulled their netting over them.

Exhausted, Kate glanced at her hammock, but she wasn't the least bit sleepy and didn't relish being curled up in the same position any longer than she needed for a good night's rest. That left her to sit by the fire until drowsiness claimed her.

"You should go to bed. We'll be up before dawn." Mr. Slader finished putting away the food supplies, then sat on a log near hers.

"I'm not sleepy. How about you?"

"The same. I told Pedro and Miguel I would take the first watch."

"When do I take a watch?"

"You don't."

"But I want to be an equal partner in this expedition," Kate said, not sure what she could do standing guard. She supposed she could scream to alert the others of danger so they would leap up and dispatch the problem. She certainly couldn't shoot anyone or anything and using a machete or knife was just as far-fetched, especially after the incident in the hallway outside Slader's room. What had she been thinking? She went out of her way not to step on bugs.

"You're the boss. That means you don't have to stand watch."

"Oh," she replied, somewhat relieved. After all, she had offered to take her turn. She couldn't help it if he didn't want her to. "I'll keep you company for a while at least."

"Afraid I'll fall asleep on duty?"

"You! Never. I don't see you shirking your duty."

He chuckled, the sound holding no humor. "You'd be surprised."

"What's that mean?"

"Nothing."

The way he said that one word made it crystal clear that topic of conversation was off-limits. But his answer only piqued her curiosity, which wasn't a good thing. That was when she got herself into trouble, and she had the funny impression she was already in enough trouble just being in the jungle.

For several minutes, Kate stared at the flames licking the logs, red, orange, yellow. The colors mesmerized her until she heard a loud roar. Heart pumping, she jumped to her feet. Then realizing what the sound was, a howler monkey, she relaxed back on her log.

"Does anything scare you?" Kate asked, amazed at how calm Mr. Slader was. He had remained on his log as though nothing had sounded.

"Yes." He took a stick and poked at the fire, sending sparks into the smoke that infused their surroundings. "I'm concerned about the men following us. The fact they are tells me everything that happened in Mandras wasn't a coincidence. Someone doesn't want you to find your brother. That leads me to the question, *why.*"

"As before, I don't have an answer for you." How many times did she have to tell him?

"You might know something that you don't realize."

"When I figure it out, I'll let you know."

"Who knew, besides General Halston, that you were coming to the Amazon?"

"Just a couple of people back in Red Creek. My pastor, whom I work for, and a neighbor who is taking care of my house."

"No one else? No one at Zach's company?"

"No one."

He threw her a puzzled look at her answer but remained quiet.

The people she knew at her brother's company wouldn't be the ones behind something like this. Mark Nelson was a childhood friend whom she'd known all her life and Chad Thomas had been her brother's roommate in college. She could still remember the crush she'd had on him and the pains she had gone through to keep it a secret from both Chad and Zach. She'd always have a special place in her heart for Chad.

The silence lengthened—long moments spent listening to the insects and animals in the jungle beyond and trying not to think one of those night creatures might be sizing her up for its next meal. So that left talking to Mr. Slader.

Sitting with him a few feet from her, she realized they were strangers who, over the next month or so, would be forced to get to know each other—well. He could talk with the Indian porters, but she couldn't even do that. Mr. Slader was all she had in the way of companionship and, being a social person, that thought frightened her. What could they possibly have in common?

Still wide awake, especially with the strange noises—thrilling, thumping, rattling—coming from the barricade of green behind her, she tried to think of something harmless to talk about. "Where are you from?" she finally asked, not a particularly original question, but it was all her tired mind could come up with.

"Mandras."

"I mean before that."

"Iquitos."

Already exasperated at his evasiveness, she said through clenched teeth, "I mean in the United States."

"Do you have anything for the sunburn on your face?"

Instead of answering him, she countered with, "Is it top secret where you came from in the States?"

"No, but I choose to keep my personal life just that. Personal."

"What's your full name?" she asked, deciding on another tactic. "What's the A. C. stand for?"

"All you need to know is Slader." He tossed the stick he had been using into the fire. "Now, do you have anything for your face?"

"Some aloe cream," she answered, peeved that something as simple as his full name was off-limits.

"Then use it tonight and tomorrow before putting on any sunscreen."

"I'm touched by your thoughtfulness."

He blinked, a frown slashing his face. "Don't be. I'll be the one who'll have to listen to you complain."

"I won't complain," she muttered, every muscle in her body taut with tension. "I was born and have only ever lived in Red Creek, Oklahoma. I haven't seen much of the world. I've been to Dallas several times, Chicago and Kansas City. That's the extent of my travels. I get the impression you've been all over the place." Not a question, but she hoped he would pick up on her topic of conversation and add something about himself.

He humphed.

"Dallas and Chicago are too big for me. Kansas City was a beautiful city, but again, too many people. That's one part of the jungle I like."

"You? I get the impression you like a lot of people around you, all talking at once."

She stiffened. "Do you always go out of your way to be—" she searched for a ladylike word to use because right now she wasn't feeling particularly ladylike "—unfriendly?"

He pointed to his chest. "This is me being friendly. I'm sitting here. I'm listening to you chatter away about cities you've been to. I call this downright congenial." He flashed her a grin that vanished immediately.

"Believe me, you won't win any congeniality contests." A big black bug, at least an inch long, crawled onto her lap. She surprised herself by remaining seated and calmly flicking it away. She wouldn't give Mr. Slader the satisfaction of another leap into the air. "I just thought that, since we're going to be spending so much time together, we would get to know each other some."

"Why?"

His question caught her off guard. Why indeed? "Are you always this difficult?" She shook her head. "Never mind answering that. You are."

"The last place I lived in the United States was Texas. There, are you satisfied?"

"Are you a big country-western music fan?"

He grimaced. "Can't stand the stuff."

"I prefer classical."

"Of course."

His tone got under her skin like the tiny fly in the jungle that burrowed into people and made them itch, a constant irritant. "What's that supposed to mean?"

"I figured you for that kind of person."

"What kind?"

"Highbrow."

"Well, for your information I also like rock and roll."

Both of his eyebrows rose. "Will wonders never cease."

Ignoring the sarcasm that was so much a part of the man, she asked, "What kind of music do you like?"

She didn't think he was going to answer, but he finally said, "Jazz. Haven't heard any in years, though."

"I don't imagine you would if the bar you hang out at is any indication of the places you visit."

"Lady, did you get a good look at Mandras? Because if you had, you'll realize there aren't a lot of places to hang out. The last time I walked the streets, I didn't see a library or an art museum."

"I saw several churches. You could always hang out there."

He surged to his feet, his hands balled at his sides. "Don't try to convert me on this trip. I know all I want to about God. I know that He…" His voice trailed off, allowing the noises from the rain forest to fill the void. "I think you'd better get some rest." He turned away, staring at the river, his stiff stance as much a barrier as the wall of jungle that surrounded them.

The fire cast his face in a red orange glow that highlighted the anger in his features. She had touched a sore subject with him, and she wondered what had happened for him to be so furious at God. Suddenly the long, bleak days ahead brightened. She had a focus other than finding her brother. She would help Mr. Slader find his way back to the Lord. Satisfied with her plan, she rose and made her way to her hammock.

After lavishing some aloe cream on her face, she gingerly lay down and pulled her mosquito netting over her. Relief from the feasting insects brought a sigh to her lips. Settling into her cotton hammock, she tried to shut out the unfamiliar sounds coming at her from all sides.

She didn't know if she would get even an hour of sleep because of her vivid imagination, which was trying to decide what was making all the unfamiliar sounds, loud whooping calls, groaning, tremulous whistles. And through all those noises droned the cicadas, a never-ending chorus. But sometime in the middle of the night she must have slept, because from deep in her dream world, a loud thunderous roar split the air. She jerked awake, her arms flailing, which sent her tumbling to the ground as she tried to get out of her hammock. The sand cushioned her fall, but the impact whooshed the air from her lungs.

Struggling to stand, she scanned the beach and found Mr. Slader already up. Another roar blasted and it sounded as though a troop of howler monkeys was right on top of them. She looked up into the trees, but it was still too dark to see much.

"Good. You're up. We'll be leaving in fifteen minutes. I want to push off at first light." Mr. Slader handed her a hat made of palm leaves, then returned to packing up.

The gift left her speechless. The hat's wide brim would adequately shade all of her face, and her neck, too. His gesture gave her hope that she would be able to reach him. *Just the sign I needed, Lord. Thank you.*

Kate felt pretty good until Mr. Slader shouted, "Get moving, lady. We have to eat, pack our things and take care of necessities all in thirteen minutes."

"Mr. Slader."

He stopped taking down his hammock and looked at her, impatience stamped in his features.

"Thank you for the hat." She smiled at him with what she hoped was a sweet expression, then set about doing what was necessary in order to be on time for their departure.

Kate had thanked him for the hat made of palm leaves as though he'd done her a favor, Slader thought an hour later on the river, not particularly pleased by the gesture. He had made it for her because he'd wanted his ball cap back. Nothing noble in that. And she had gone and made a big deal out of it. Worse, he was now thinking of her as *Kate*. He didn't want to do that. He needed to keep his distance.

Just as he thought that, she tapped him on the shoulder. He gritted his teeth and glanced back at her in the canoe.

She held up a tube of sunscreen. "Do you want some?"

"No," he bit out, and resumed his vigil, facing forward. He didn't want to look at her pink-flushed cheeks, her large soulful eyes hidden only partially under the palm hat.

He paddled harder, forcing his body to the limit, determined to put as much distance between them and their pursuers. He could almost feel the people behind them closing in. And if they did, he couldn't count on Miguel and Pedro if they had to fight. They had a reputation of fleeing at the first sight of real trouble. It would be him against four others. Not good odds, especially with Kate in the middle.

There he went again. Thinking of her as *Kate*. Thinking of her period! If only he hadn't been at the Blue Dolphin when she had walked into it. But then that would have left her at the bar alone and that wouldn't have been good for her. He knew some of the men who frequented the place. Disreputable men who took without asking. He was beginning to wonder if she had nine lives like a cat. If so, she had used up two so far. And he didn't want to be around when the ninth one came due. He would *not* be responsible for another woman's death. Period!

Then why was he paddling furiously up a river with four men following who meant to do Kate harm? That led him back to the question: why had he agreed to guide her in the first place? He didn't understand his behavior of the past few days, which really bothered him above everything else. He had fallen into a pattern where he only looked out for himself and now he was responsible for a woman again. Now he had promised to do something he wasn't sure was a good idea—go into Quentas territory to find her brother whom Slader didn't think was alive.

"Mr. Slader?"

"Just Slader," he practically growled at her. A picture of her mouth with full lips made for pouting popped into his brain. He shoved it away.

For a few heartbeats she didn't say anything, then she spoke. "I wanted to thank you again for this hat. It's great. It shades more than my face."

"I didn't do it for you. I wanted my hat back." There, that would set the record straight.

"Well, whatever your reason for taking the time to make it, I really appreciate it."

He clamped his jaw hard—so hard, pain streaked down his neck. He put more force behind his paddling.

"I'll have to return the favor. You're sure you don't want any sunscreen?"

He nodded, afraid to say anything. She was way too cheery so early in the morning with men on their tail. The hairs at the nape of his neck tingled and this time it wasn't because he knew she was staring at his back. In his gut he felt Slick and his pals were closing in.

"I'm quite an accomplished singer. At least that's what everyone at my church says. I could always sing some songs to pass our time. Sort of like our very own radio. Would you like me to—"

"No," he cut her off, but he was proud that his voice was amazingly calm considering the emotions churning in his stomach. He could imagine the type of songs she sang, especially if the people at her church were the ones to tell her she could sing well. He wanted none of that.

He'd spent many Sundays in church while growing up and going to college and it hadn't gotten him anywhere. God had still let him down when he had needed Him the most. No sir, he did not want to hear Miss Prim and Proper sing some church song. That would be all he needed to really make this day one he regretted waking up to.

Over and over he dipped his paddle into the muddy

water, willing them to move faster. But the jungle didn't pass by quickly enough for his peace of mind. He wanted to rub at his neck to rid himself of the nagging feeling that they were in trouble, but he didn't dare stop paddling.

Suddenly the air split with an alien sound. He tensed.

SEVEN

Kate paused whistling "When the Saints Go Marching In" to take a deep breath. Mr. Slader twisted around and gave her a glare that could freeze a pan of boiling water.

"What do you think you're doing?" he asked in a steely, quiet voice. His face had actually turned a deep shade of red.

"Whistling a tune. I thought that was obvious."

"I thought I said no music."

He was pronouncing his words slowly again, and Kate had to fight her irritation from taking over. She was determined to win him to her way of thinking, not alienate him further. "No singing. You didn't say anything about whistling," she said in a level voice. "I've got to do something to break up the monotony."

"Well, get used to it. That's traveling in the jungle. No more singing, whistling or anything remotely related to music. In fact, lady, no sound at all."

"You're banning me from talking?"

"Yes." He resumed paddling as if he were wrestling with the water.

Stunned by his overbearing manner, which she should be used to by now, she asked, "Why?"

"Because I've got an itch."

"Then scratch yourself. I realize the insects are bad, but we don't have to stop talking because of them." With all the talk of insects and itching, Kate found herself rubbing the palm of her hand along her forearm where several bugs had fed on her earlier. She had a cluster of red bumps as proof.

"Are you really that naive?" He shook his head. "People are right behind us. I don't want to draw any more attention to us than is absolutely necessary. Understand?"

He was back to speaking in the voice where he said each word one slow syllable at a time, and that riled her. Honestly, she had tried to remain calm and cool, but she only had so much patience.

She wasn't a worldly person. She knew that, but all he'd had to do was explain to her why he wanted her to be quiet and she would comply. She had started to tell him just that when he said something to the porters, then directed the canoe toward shore. The urgency in his voice alerted Kate that something wasn't right. She straightened and glanced around, especially downriver. Nothing.

When she looked at the tangle of green they headed toward, she couldn't see where they would land their craft. The greenery was impregnable and a couple of stories high. On closer inspection, she saw a large log jutting out into the water and wondered why Mr. Slader was stopping now, especially if their pursuers were getting nearer. But she didn't say anything. She was still recovering from his last icy glare and sarcastic comment about how naive she was.

Pedro, in front, tied the canoe to the log, then hopped onto it. Mr. Slader turned to her and motioned for her to follow suit. She crawled toward Pedro, who extended his hand. She gingerly made her way to the fallen tree trunk, which wasn't as wide as she had originally thought.

On her hands and knees she inched along the log toward the wall of green, with Pedro leading the way and Mr. Slader and Miguel behind her dragging the canoe from the river. She sensed the impatience in Mr. Slader, but there was no way she would hurry herself. Just one glance at the muddy water with green plants and mangled, twisted branches below its surface gave her a creepy feeling that caused goose bumps to erupt all over her.

She finally made it to the dense undergrowth, and Pedro pulled her into the brush after him. Limbs scratched at her skin, and a branch struck her in the face as she went deeper into the green barrier. She slowed her pace. Mr. Slader pushed on her back and sent her forward into another green obstacle, this one with thorns that tore into her flesh. Rivulets of blood trickled down her exposed forearm where her shirt was ripped.

Mr. Slader and Miguel carried the canoe past her to the left and thrust the craft into a thick barricade of undergrowth. Then Mr. Slader grabbed her and yanked her down.

She had started to protest the manhandling when he

clamped a hand over her mouth and, close to her ear, whispered, "Quiet." He motioned toward the river.

Through a small opening in the sea of green, Kate spied a canoe passing their hiding place, no more than twenty yards away, close enough for her to see Slick and another man, as well as their *big* guns strapped across their backs. They were traveling fast.

Fear clawed at her as the branches had only seconds before. Her heart stopped for several beats, or at least that was the way it seemed to her. Her chest constricted with each breath she dragged in. Her world spun before her eyes. She clutched some of the brush to keep herself upright.

Her pursuers had only been minutes behind them. Their only saving grace had been the many twists and turns in the river. That itch Mr. Slader spoke of was dead on.

Hey, hadn't Mr. Slader said something about four men? Kate studied the last bend in the river downstream, waiting for the other two to appear. No one else followed.

A good fifteen minutes passed before Mr. Slader signaled that they could move about. Kate pushed to her feet, aware that the greenery encircling her was like a cocoon wrapped about her.

She rolled her shoulders and twisted at the waist. "Where are the other two men?" she asked Mr. Slader, his features set in a scowl as he continued to stare at the river.

"That's a good question. I'm guessing Slick posted

them where they spent the night to prevent us from doubling back to Mandras anytime soon."

"Which was what you had been thinking of doing when you first saw Slick?"

"Yep. It's nice to see we're beginning to understand each other."

"I understand you very well, Mr. Slader."

"If you don't stop calling me *Mr. Slader,* men posted or not we'll be going back to Mandras."

His stare drilled into her with an intensity that made his point clear. "I'll stop if you'll stop calling me *lady.* My name is *Kate.*" She stuck out her hand. "Deal?"

"It's a deal, *Kate.*" He shook her hand once, then quickly released it.

Kate wasn't sure why her heart began beating fast. Because he'd said her first name or because he'd touched her in a simple handshake? Either way, the harsh climate was playing havoc with her senses if she was letting something like that make her heart pound. Really! Most people called her *Kate* and she had certainly been touched by a man before. For that matter, Mr.—no, just Slader, had touched her before.

Rubbing her two palms together, she asked, "What do we do now? Two men are downstream and two upstream."

Slader motioned with his head in the direction away from the river. "We go thataway."

Kate examined where he indicated, feet and feet of lianas, branches, knots and tendrils all forming an intricate network of flora. "But how? It's a wall of green."

He placed his hand on the hilt of his machete. "That's

why we brought these. There's often thick underbrush near the river, but farther inland it shouldn't be as bad."

After Slader and the porters hid the canoe, Slader and Pedro took their machetes and began hacking through the snarl. Miguel stood behind her as though he was guarding the rear. That thought sent a shiver down her spine. Just half an hour ago, men had passed them on the river—men who wanted to do her harm.

Kate scanned the area around her. In less than two days in the jungle she was beginning to hate the color green. "Do you know where you're going—Slader?" It felt so alien not to call him *mister.*

In the lead, Slader paused in swinging his machete and threw her a glance over his shoulder. "Aren't you asking that question a little late in the game?"

She pursed her mouth. "I mean, how can you tell where to go? Everything looks the same." She waved her hand in front of her face, feeling as if the green barrier were closing in on her. Having a touch of claustrophobia didn't help, either. "There isn't a trail to follow."

"This isn't a nice little park in the United States with trails laid out for the weekend camper." He pulled a round, shiny disk out of his pocket and flipped it open. "But if it will make you feel any better, I have a GPS and I know the general area where your brother became lost."

"General, as in…?"

He laughed. "La—Kate, has anyone ever told you that you have lousy timing? No matter what I answer it doesn't make any difference. You're going where I go. End of story."

He pivoted and resumed cutting a path through the dense foliage, the sound of his machete seeming unusually loud. What if Slick came back and heard them hacking their way through the jungle? She peered back, her gaze falling upon Miguel, who offered a smile. No one else seemed concerned. Or perhaps more importantly, they realized there wasn't a choice but to go through the thick jungle, which meant cutting their way with the machetes.

Okay, so maybe he had a point. She certainly wasn't going to hang around the river hoping some friendly person would come along to take her upriver. She was stuck with Mr. Slader.

He was stuck with Kate, Slader thought, flinging down his backpack to the forest floor five hours later. Even if he wanted to and could take her back to Mandras, they were trapped and the only feasible course of action was to move forward and hope they found her brother with a large, friendly tribe of Indians to help them. She insisted he was alive, and Slader hoped he was because otherwise the odds were against them making it back to civilization in one piece. Double-checking his shotgun, the only weapon besides their knives and machetes they had, he refused to think about what would happen to Kate if she were caught by the men following them.

Kate shrugged out of her pack and collapsed down beside it, her body hugging it, her arms wrapped around the canvas as though she were a flower that had wilted in on itself. Sweat soaked her white shirt, the sleeves rolled up to her elbows, and her tan slacks were torn and dirty. If he hadn't known better, he would have thought she had gone swimming in the river. When he peered down at his own pants and shirt, he realized he wasn't much better off. He could imagine what she thought of his attire. This was a woman who didn't go camping, didn't like to be without her little "civilized luxuries"—soap, daily change of clothing, shower.

Which meant Kate loved her brother very much if she was willing to suffer such indignities. Slader settled next to his backpack. He'd never tell her, but he admired her for the kind of love that had sent her thousands of miles from home into an unknown environment so totally different from what she was used to to rescue a man who was probably dead. He didn't think his sister would cross the street to save his sorry soul. Until he'd met his wife, Renee, he hadn't known what love really was. She'd shown him, giving him a glimpse into a world he'd never be a part of again. He'd never put himself into that kind of position because when she had died, she had taken part of him with her—his heart.

He glanced over at Kate, who was still cradling her backpack, her eyes closed, the hat he had made her lying on the ground next to her. He couldn't think about Renee. He didn't want to go through painful memories, and yet Kate brought all those remembrances to the foreground. What was it about her that reminded him of his wife? They certainly didn't look anything alike. Renee had been drop-dead gorgeous with long blond hair and green eyes that a man could get lost in. She had been nearly six feet tall, not a petite little thing like Kate. And Renee hadn't had an ounce of extra fat on her.

They had one thing in common, though: their deep devotion to the Lord. That devotion had drawn Slader to Renee. But that love of God hadn't saved his wife in the end. She'd been taken, along with his unborn child.

"Is something wrong—Slader?"

He snapped his head around. "What could be wrong? I personally love running for my life. How about you?" Why did she make him feel as though she could see into his soul with her big, blue eyes.

"Besides that." She slowly rose to a sitting position wincing as if the effort was almost too much. "Is anything else wrong? You looked—upset. More than usual."

He wasn't going to get into his personal life with her. Instead, he said, "Slick will realize we aren't on the river and backtrack. I'm hoping it takes him a while to discover that little fact. But you can't count on it, especially the way things have been going."

"He doesn't know where we're going. We cut our own path through the jungle back there."

"That path can be found and many people in the area know the general location of where your brother went down. He'll assume that's where we're heading."

"Okay. But you said yourself that location was a large area."

"Slick's been down here a few years, making quite

an unsavory reputation for himself. He knows this area almost as well as I do."

Kate brought her knees up to her chest and clasped her legs. "Is this where we're camping tonight?"

"Yes." Slader spoke to Miguel and Pedro, giving them instructions about setting up the camp, then he turned back to Kate and said, "Hang your hammock, then gather firewood. I'm going to scout the area and look for food. Pedro is staying in camp. Miguel is going out to hunt for food, too." He rose.

After watching Slader disappear from view, Kate examined the shadowy jungle floor, then the huge trees jutting upward with lianas hanging down from the canopy above as though they were thick cables dangling to the ground. Little sunlight bled through the green ceiling above them, making it seem as if it were perpetual dusk. But below, it was relatively free of vegetation, making their progress the past few hours easier than when they'd first had to hack their way through thick brush near the river.

She looked down at her slacks, torn in places as though the jungle had clawed at her the whole way, trying to keep her from going forward. If it weren't for the insects, she'd consider cutting the pants off above the knees. At least for the past couple of hours she hadn't had to worry about getting sunburned.

But still the dark shadows about her gave her imagination a field day. Anyone could be lurking behind one of those big tree trunks, readying himself to jump out when they least expected it.

She placed her hands on the spongy ground of

decaying matter to help herself stand. Before she had a chance to gather her energy to lumber to her feet, something crawled across her wrist. She let out a squeak and leaped up, shaking both of her hands and stamping her feet. Peering down, she saw a line of ants carrying torn leaves. Her shoulders slumped forward in relief.

Not everything in the rain forest was scary and bad. In fact, very few animals and insects in all the ones who populated the jungle were. Well, one good thing about the ants was she was on her feet and ready to collect the firewood. Without their "help" she might have still been on the ground contemplating getting up. They also got her blood pumping through her body. Sucking in a deep breath of the moisture-laden air, she closed her eyes for a few seconds. A calmness descended.

That calmness lasted the whole way through picking up pieces of wood for the fire. It disappeared the second she saw Slader return to the camp. Again her heart began to beat too fast and she found herself breathing shallow, quick gulps of air. He was so different from any man she'd known. He didn't live by the same rules as she did. She hurriedly turned away, searching for that serenity she'd possessed only a moment before.

On the top of his backpack, he placed some strange-looking pieces of...she guessed fruit but she wasn't really sure. When he straightened, he surveyed the campsite.

"You weren't gone long," she managed to say. Why couldn't he have taken a little longer? This tense nervousness was wearing her down. *Lord, help me. I'm*

wound as tight as a spring. I can't keep this up or I'm
afraid something will give.

"This breadfruit wasn't too far. But I found something I want to show you. Bring some soap and
shampoo if you have it."

"Soap? Shampoo?" She stood still, not sure she'd
heard him correctly. Both those items sounded wonderful.

"Hurry. It won't be light much longer." Slader bent
and rummaged through his pack until he found his
flashlight. He started back the way he'd come.

Kate stared at his retreating figure for a few seconds
longer before she set in motion. Soap usually meant
cleaning something. She was hoping it was herself that
she would be cleaning. With that thought, she rushed
after Slader before the jungle swallowed him up and
she lost sight of him.

Slader heard Kate trampling behind him as though
she were a herd of wild peccaries racing toward the
river with a jaguar on their tail. He smiled at that
picture. At least any animal nearby would hear her and
get out of her way.

When he arrived at a creek that ran through the
jungle, he stopped at its bank and waited for Kate.
Twenty yards upstream the creek formed a pool that
was so clear he could see its bottom, three or four feet
down. Perfect to wash off in, he had thought when
he'd discovered it.

He was beginning to regret the impulse. He should
have hunted for more food. He should have scouted the

area better. But no, instead he had bolted back to Kate so fast that it could have made a person's head spin. She would read the wrong thing into this, he was sure of that.

He should forget—

"A creek! Where does it go?"

Her question interrupted his momentary panic. "To the river." He pointed toward the way they had come earlier that day. "Eventually."

"I mean this way," she said, gesturing in the opposite direction.

He shrugged. He could still get out of this and not show her the pool. But when she stepped to the bank of the creek and knelt to cup the water, her sighs as she splashed the cool liquid onto her face caused him to say, "There's a pool not far from here." The second he finished the treacherous declaration he clamped his jaw shut, hoping any further revelations would stay in his thoughts only.

"A pool." She practically breathed the word on another sigh of contentment. "Will it be safe to wash in?"

Rising next to him, she toweled her wet face with the sleeve of her dirty, sweaty shirt, leaving a streak of mud on her cheek. She had come a long way from the woman he had first met at the Blue Dolphin, her dress neat and clean, her hair pulled back in a tight bun. Now her auburn tresses were tied up in a ponytail with a wisp of curls framing her face. Her cheeks and forehead were sunburned. He wondered what her hair would look like down about her shoulders.

Whoa, there. Don't go down that road. His panic returned full-fledged as he strode toward the pool with visions of Kate, her hair down, her face scrubbed clean, her eyes shining in delight.

He was so absorbed in his fantasy he nearly stumbled over a root in the path. He caught himself before falling, then banished any thoughts of Kate other than as Miss Prim and Proper to the dark reaches of his mind, never to be uncovered again—if he knew what was best for him.

Her squeal of joy made a mockery of his promise to himself, especially when he pivoted toward her and found her pulling out the band that held up her ponytail. Her hair fell about her shoulders in a mass of reddish brown curls that were in direct contradiction to the woman she presented to the world. Her brown hair, seared with a touch of fire, gave a hint of her true personality, which he suspected she kept bottled up inside, much like her tresses bound in its severe bun. He stared at her, hoping his mouth wasn't hanging open.

"This is perfect. Thank you. Thank you. This is the best gift you could have given me."

He had known she would do this and still he had brought her to the pool. "It's nothing," he grumbled, frowning at the idea she had thought he had given her a gift—as a friend would. No, they were not friends. They were worlds apart. He wouldn't go back to her world and she would never stay in his.

Kate walked partway around the pool, peering into the water as though making sure what lay beneath was harmless. "Do you think it's safe enough for me to go in totally, not just wash up on the bank?"

The tumble of her fiery-colored hair hid her face from him, but he could imagine her teeth nibbling at her full lower lip, as she so often did when perplexed about something or worried. "Yes. If you want, I'll go in with you or I can stand at the edge and keep guard."

She turned toward him, the light streaming through the trees catching her face just right. How had he ever thought she was plain? She tilted her head and contemplated his offer.

"I have plenty of soap. I can share it with you."

He chuckled. "Is that your not-so-subtle way of telling me I stink?"

She laughed, a warm, light sound that permeated the area, prodding him to join in her merriment. "No, but I thought, like me, you might enjoy cleaning up. We have no idea when we'll have another chance."

"True." He removed his shoes and socks.

For a brief second Kate's eyes grew round. "What are you doing?"

"I don't care to get my tennis shoes any wetter than they already are, but I suppose my socks could use a washing."

"Oh," she said simply as she took off her shoes and socks, too.

"I'm not taking off anything else, la—Kate. You don't have to worry."

"I wasn't—okay, I thought you were going to."

"It doesn't take a rocket scientist to know you've led a very sheltered life when it comes to men."

She blushed, her cheeks reddening even more beneath her sunburn. She averted her face.

"Believe me. You're perfectly safe with me."

She jerked around. "Have you just insulted me?"

He started to give her a sarcastic retort, then realized he didn't want to because he did respect her beliefs. In today's society, a woman like Kate was rare to find. He was just beginning to realize that about her. "No, I think I'm paying you a compliment."

Surprise flitted across her face before a brilliant smile graced her lips. "Thanks. Can I ask a favor?"

He nodded.

"Will you go in first?" she asked, clutching her bar of soap and washcloth in her hands.

He checked the pool in front of him before diving into it and coming up halfway across. He stood and the water came to his lower chest. "It feels great. You'd better hurry." He glanced toward the sky. "We don't have long before it gets dark."

She followed suit, slicing through the water and emerging a few feet from him. "Oh, you're so right. This is wonderful."

"Just remember you said that when you start arguing with me later."

"That it's wonderful or you're right?" The imp stared at him.

He dragged his hand across the top of the pool, sending water spraying into her face. "That I am right. That's important to remember."

"Oh, you are?" She splashed him back, her giggles peppering the air.

He dove beneath the water and came toward her. She backed away, but he pursued her, gaining on her rapidly.

Putting her hand out in front to stop him, he grabbed it and tugged her beneath the pool. He came up for air at the same time she did, spluttering, flailing her arms.

"Where's the soap?" she asked, the washcloth still grasped in one hand.

Knowing the importance of it to Kate, he immediately said, "I'll find it." He went back under the water and searched the bottom. He did that three times before announcing, "I can't find it."

She smiled sweetly and produced it from her pocket. "Oh, I seem to have found it."

He stalked toward her.

She held up her hand, taking a step back. "Remember it's getting late. We need to wash up and get back to camp."

"You weren't too worried about the time when I was looking for the soap," he mumbled, but halted.

Quickly she lathered her washcloth, then passed him the bar. "Well, I am now."

He watched her run the cloth over her face and neck, along the expose skin on her arms. He did likewise, using the suds in his hands. When she took the soap back, she began washing her clothes while still wearing them, as well as her socks, then his socks at the side of the pool. That touched him more than he wanted to acknowledge. He couldn't remember someone doing a chore like that for him in a long time.

When she was through washing, she gave him the soap again to use. He took care of his clothes as best he could while still wearing them. He would have to be satisfied with this partial cleanup.

While he finished up with his clothes, Kate pulled a small bottle from her pocket and poured some pink liquid into her hand. "Do you want some shampoo?"

With a nod, he held out his palm while she gave him some, then put the bottle back into her pocket. The scent of roses drifted to him. He almost rinsed the shampoo off in the pool without using it, but he knew his hair needed a washing, too, even if he would smell like a rose garden. Untying the leather strap that tied his long hair at the nape of his neck, he massaged the pink liquid into his scalp, then dunked down into the pool.

When he resurfaced, he saw Kate with her eyes closed running her fingers through her sudsy strands. The scent of roses overpowered every other smell, and the pure beauty of seeing such enjoyment on her features sucker punched him. He looked away as though he had intruded on a private moment he didn't have a right to see.

But he heard her enjoyment at being able to wash the sweat and grime from her hair. Each sound sent a longing through him that took him by surprise. His life was far from ideal, but it was the life he had chosen for himself. Suddenly he questioned that choice. Anger swelled to the surface, and he directed it at Kate, the woman who made him doubt himself.

"We need to get back to camp. Now!" Although he faced away from her, he sensed her disbelief at his sharp tone.

A sound of splashing greeted his order, and he looked over his shoulder to see her emerge from beneath the pool and shake her head. Water sprayed everywhere. Her gaze locked with his, a hurt look in their blue depths that she hurriedly masked by dropping her eyelids. When she peered at him again a few seconds later, there wasn't a bit of emotion in her expression, which was quite unusual for her. Most of the time he could read, on her face, every feeling flitting through her mind. Suddenly he regretted his harshness and started to apologize.

She waded past him, looking toward shore and the quickly growing darkness of the surrounding rain forest. "Don't just stand there. We need to get moving. Isn't that what you said?"

"Yes." This woman was playing mind games. He didn't know if he was coming or going half the time and he didn't like it one bit.

By the time he had put his shoes back on without his socks, the dark shadows had closed in on them. They had stayed too long. He found his flashlight and said, "Stay right behind me. Step where I step. In fact, put your hand on my shoulder."

She sucked in a sharp breath, but she did as he asked.

The feel of her hand burned into his shoulder. He flicked on the flashlight and determinedly focused on the path before him, not on the woman behind him dogging his every step as he had commanded.

Going swimming had not been his wisest move, he decided as he fumbled around in the dark jungle. The light before him marginally showed the way. He had allowed Kate's wishes to influence him. He took a deep, fortifying breath and the smell of roses accosted him. Roses! What man wore the scent of roses?

Through the darkness he saw the fire that Pedro and Miguel had started. He hastened his pace, needing to distance himself from Kate as quickly as possible. Her presence behind him, her constant touch, was driving him crazy with thoughts of smelling like a rose garden and kissing the woman senseless as he ran his hands through the wild mane that was loose about her shoulders.

Sitting across from the fire, with Slader as far away as possible and still be in camp, Kate wondered what had changed on the walk back from the creek. They had actually been on friendly terms—almost downright playful—for a while back at the pool. Now he hardly said a word to her, and when she caught him staring at her, he immediately looked away. They were back to being strangers and she wasn't sure what had happened to change that. If only she had more experience dealing with men, then maybe she could figure it out.

As before, Pedro and Miguel went to bed first because they were taking the second and third watches. Slader remained across from her, drawing circles in the dirt with a stick as if he had nothing better to do. A roar penetrated the constant jungle noise. Kate tensed.

"A jaguar," Slader said, cutting the silence between them for the first time since they had returned from the pool. "Probably a male defending his territory."

"Something the male of the species does a lot," she couldn't resist interjecting into the conversation.

"They are solitary creatures with a large territory."

"Sounds like someone I know."

"Meaning?"

"You've made it abundantly clear you like being a loner." She swept her arm across her body. "And you've got the whole jungle as your—territory."

A high-pitched squeal pierced the air. "I think he found his dinner."

"Survival of the fittest." Kate stared into the low flames of the fire.

"The law of the jungle."

"What happens if those men catch up with us?" She shivered when she thought about Slick and the time he had trapped her in the alley. If it hadn't been for Slader, no telling what would have happened to her.

"The strongest and smartest will survive, and I intend for that to be us, Kate."

The steel thread in his voice caused her to shiver again.

"But I'm banking on not being caught by Slick and his pals. If we stay ahead of them, then we avoid a fight, which is a much safer plan."

"Zach will be able to help when we find him. He has a black belt in karate."

"Which won't do him much good against a gun." He paused a few seconds, then asked, "What will you do if you don't find Zach? We can't wander around in this jungle forever. Have you thought about how long you'll search before you call it quits?"

She gripped her hands together, twisting them over and over. "No. We *will* find him. I have trust in God that this will not remain unresolved."

"I hope your God doesn't let you down."

"He won't."

Slader shook his head, shoving to his feet. "Get some sleep, Kate. Tomorrow we have to put distance between us and Slick." He walked away, stopping at the edge of the jungle and staring into the darkness.

Kate observed him for a few minutes, realizing the second she had mentioned the Lord he had shut down. Her plan to show him the power and love of God wouldn't be easy to accomplish. But she hadn't expected it to be. The reward would be worth it in the end.

Deciding to take him up on his suggestion to get some sleep, Kate stood and stretched. She ached all over, but the swim earlier and the opportunity to clean up had been wonderful and refreshing beyond her wildest dreams. She was still surprised that Slader had shown her the pool and given her the chance to wash herself. Like making her the palm hat, the gesture spoke of a facet he tried to hide, but she saw through his tough facade to the man she suspected he had tried to conceal from others, a man who had somehow been hurt deeply and had banished himself to the ends of the earth—as a form of penance?

She made her way to her hammock and removed her shoes. One pair of her socks was still drying by the fire and the other she would wear tomorrow. She knew she was already getting a blister from the short walk back from the pool without her socks on and that wouldn't do with all the hiking they had ahead of them. If she had to crawl, she would not hold up this expedition.

After lining up her boots below her hammock, a luxury she hadn't done the night before because she'd fallen asleep with them on, she slipped beneath her netting and curled up into a ball. She wore her clean shirt while her other one was also drying by the fire next to her torn khakis. She now wore a pair of jeans, her only other pants. Its thick material was a better shield against insect bites but was much hotter than her khakis. At least she had on dry clothes. In Red Creek she had taken clean, dry clothes for granted. Not anymore.

Listening to the increasingly familiar sounds of the jungle about her, she relaxed her tense muscles. Sleep came rapidly.

The spatter of water in her face brought Kate out of a deep dreamless state. She blinked her eyes open and realized rain was falling from the canopy of trees above her. The fire was low, giving off little light, but she didn't need to see the rain. It pelted her with increasing force. She came up out of the hammock, remembering to swing her legs over the side so she wouldn't tumble to the jungle floor like she had the day before.

She reached for her backpack and drew out her poncho. After shrugging into it, she looked about her and found Slader stirring in his hammock. He sat up, his focus zeroing in on her. He, too, put on his rain gear.

Kate had begun to slide her feet into her boots when Slader shouted above the sound of the rain, "Don't."

"Why not?"

"Check your boots first. Some critters like to hide in them."

Kate nearly dropped the boot she held. She turned it over and shook it. A spider crawled out and descended to the ground. She quickly did the same with the other boot, then gingerly put her sock-clad foot into it, hoping there were no more little creatures inside.

As she laced up her boots, she watched Slader circling the middle of the camp, his frown evolving into a scowl. He muttered something she couldn't fully hear and was probably glad she didn't.

"What's wrong?" She stood and looked about, too.

"Pedro and Miguel are gone."

EIGHT

"They can't be," Kate exclaimed, taking in the place where Miguel had slung his hammock. The empty spot made a mockery of her words. She scanned the area where Pedro had hung his hammock. It, too, was gone. "Why?"

Slader continued to search the campsite, his expression growing more ominous with each second that passed. "They helped themselves to the extra supplies and my shotgun. It looks like all we have left is our own backpacks."

"I guess we should be grateful they left us that." Kate sank down onto the log near the dying fire, shielding her head with the hood on the poncho. "What do we do now?"

Slader untied his wet hammock and stuffed it into his backpack. "We keep going. We don't have a choice. Come on. I want to get moving as soon as it's light enough to."

"It's obvious Pedro and Miguel don't feel they owe us any loyalty."

"Which means if Slick finds them they won't keep quiet. Or Slick's somehow behind them leaving."

Slader's words heightened the sense of danger. Kate surveyed the dark jungle as though it were a menacing being; she wondered if Slick was out there watching them. If he was, she would go down fighting, she decided. Quickly she pushed to her feet and took down her hammock. As she put it into her pack, she wished yet again that she had carried more of the supplies, especially the food.

When she returned to Red Creek, she intended to lift weights. She would never put herself in this position again—depending on others. Her stomach tightened with hunger, but she didn't say anything, knowing how limited their food supply was. *Lord, please help us to find my brother but also something to eat. I'd even eat a fish gladly. And, Lord, please send Slick in the opposite direction.*

After Slader had cleared away all evidence that they had camped there, he indicated that Kate should follow him. Even though it was after sunrise, the jungle remained dark from the rain and the high canopy that blocked so much of the light even on a bright sunny day. He used his flashlight to help guide him. Kate mirrored his steps, the bottom half of her totally soaked and muddy in a short time.

Wet, hungry and miserable, she refused to complain to Slader. He couldn't be any better off. They were in this together which, surprisingly, made her feel better. If she had to have anyone on her side, Slader would be the first person she would pick. In his presence, she felt safe, even though she knew people were after her and possibly not far behind them.

Seven hours later, it was still raining. Kate placed one foot in front of the other, forcing herself to keep going. The sloshing of her steps sounded over the rain striking the trees and falling to the jungle floor. She needed to rest, but she bit down hard to keep the request inside.

Ever since they had left the camp earlier that morning, Slader had been driving them both hard to get as far away from where they had been the night before as possible. He hadn't said more than a few words to her and what little they had eaten—a banana and something that was supposed to be beef stew in a pouch— had been consumed while they had walked.

Lord. Help! I don't think I can do this.

A few minutes later, Slader came to an abrupt halt under a large tree with a thick canopy of leaves that sheltered them partially from the continuous rain. He slipped his backpack off, then turned to her to help her remove hers.

"We'll take a twenty-minute break."

Thank You. Thank You, Lord.

Ignoring the fact that the ground ran with muddy rivulets, Kate sank down onto her waterproof backpack and used it as a seat cushion. She couldn't stand another second. She spread her poncho over her wet jeans to give her some relief even though she realized it wouldn't really make any difference. Soaked to the bone was soaked to the bone.

Slader squatted a foot away from her, staring out into the gray jungle, his eyes intense as if he expected someone to appear any minute. That thought scared her. As he had on the river, did he sense people behind them?

"Do you have an itch?" she asked.

He shook his head. "But don't think they aren't out there, because they are. That's why we can only stop for a little while. This rain is miserable but it does wash our steps away."

Then thank You, Lord, for the rain.

"So it could be worse," Kate said.

He swiveled his attention to her. "Yes, I guess it could, Miss Pollyanna."

"I prefer to think of the glass as half full, not half empty."

"Somehow I figured that. Not always a good thing when you're running for your life."

"How often have you run for your life?"

He shrugged, his expression darkening with emotion for a brief moment. "A few times."

"This is my first and I hope, last time."

"The thing about life is that we don't always know what's gonna happen."

"I feel pretty sure that in Red Creek, I won't have to worry about running for my life."

His chuckle vied with the sound of the rain. "Most of my life I've lived in a jungle or a big city. It's a definite possibility either place. Actually, it is anywhere."

Cynicism stamped his features with a scowl, making

Kate sad. What had made him that way? There was so much to be thankful for. "It's obvious that we have had different life experiences. I won't say that Red Creek isn't without its crime. Just last summer, the gas station was robbed and someone stole the clothes off Mrs. Radisson's clothesline. Justin Black drinks too much on Saturday nights and ends up causing a disturbance. And the teenagers go too fast in their cars down some of the residential streets."

Slader again searched the surrounding rain forest. "I can see that your sheriff is busy."

The sardonic tone to his voice didn't upset her. She'd come to learn that was Slader's way. "I'm thankful there's still a place like Red Creek left to live."

His gaze returned to hers. "Actually, so am I."

"You are?"

"I can't see you anyplace but somewhere like Red Creek."

"True. This trip has shown me a whole different side to life."

"The underside."

She laughed, liking the thought that she could laugh after the day they had put in. "Yes, and something more than that. There's a beauty in the jungle that I'll never find in Red Creek. The rain forest is raw and primitive, but it's life at its more elemental."

"That survival of the fittest we talked about?"

"Sometimes. But have you noticed how God has balanced out things? Even the most vulnerable animals have defense mechanisms in place. Look at a rabbit. Fair game for many predators, but God has given the rabbit speed, as well as the ability to reproduce in great numbers."

"But then man has stepped into the picture and upset that balance. You see a lot of that imbalance in play in the jungle now. That's why the Quentas have kept themselves hidden from the rest of the world and so far, they have been pretty successful."

Kate shifted on her backpack. "Do you think that Zach made contact with them?"

"Isn't it a little late to wonder about that? We're going on the assumption he did and that they won't welcome us with spears and arrows."

"It's hard to believe in today's time that there are places still isolated from the world."

"Not many, but where the Quentas reside it's very isolated, partially due to the terrain, partially due to their reputation."

She trembled. "Are you trying to scare me?"

"Is it working? Are you ready to call it quits?"

"No, never. Not until I know what has happened to Zach."

He twisted about to face her. "You've got me for a few more weeks. That's all. Then we'll have to call it quits." He gestured toward the drenched jungle. "This is just a small sampling of what the rainy season is like."

Kate only half heard what he had said after, "You've got me." Her mind fixated on those words, and a picture of him and her together beyond the present flirted with her equilibrium. *My, where had that image of them come from?* Panic festered in her stomach, causing it to churn.

Amazed that she could react more intensely to the idea of a relationship with Slader than the fierce Quentas, who at this very moment could be watching them, she swallowed several times and said, "I won't leave until I know."

"Has anyone told you that you're one stubborn woman?"

"A few have mentioned that trait."

Rising in one fluid motion, Slader extended his hand to her. "Well, then we'd better get moving if we're going to find that brother of yours."

She fitted her hand into his and let him pull her up, every muscle in her body protesting that they were heading out again. "Do you think this rain will stop anytime soon?"

"It might, then it might not."

She laughed. "A definitive answer."

"It's the only kind you can give when it comes to rain and the jungle." He slung his backpack over his shoulders, then helped her put hers on.

As Kate trailed behind Slader, she thought about their short break. Something had changed again with them. It was nothing she could put her finger on, but more a gut feeling. It was almost as though they were no longer guide and client, but a true team.

Rain pounded down on Kate as they emerged from the thick jungle into an area more open to the sky. The uneven terrain headed upward, and her calves quivered with exhaustion. The roar of water sounded in the distance.

"Are we near a river?"

"Yes, a small one. It marks the Quentas territory. I haven't been beyond it. Not many have."

Excitement, mixed with a healthy respect for the danger before them, took hold of Kate. It might not be long before she found Zach.

"We'll cross above the waterfall."

Hence the reason they were climbing up the steep incline. She could do this.

"But we'll wait till tomorrow to do it."

Getting a face full of rain, Kate looked up at the sky, dark with clouds and the approaching sunset. Following a path that curved around the side of a cliff, she stayed close behind Slader, only a few feet separating them. She wasn't afraid of heights, but it was a long way down. Tops of trees lay to her right, like a green carpet. Zach was somewhere out there beneath those trees. Despite the arduous task before her, her excitement gave her the energy to do what was needed.

Near the top of the precipitous slope they had ascended, Slader paused to get his bearings. Kate did, too. Turning slightly on the trail, she faced the sea of treetops, a gray mist interwoven in the green. Off to the west, the rain had stopped and orange strips ribboned the blue sky like a woven tapestry.

"This is beautiful," Kate said as the rain pummeled her. Although the weather promised to clear soon, the downpour continued, its intensity increasing, masking the sound of the waterfall.

"Let's go. We'll be cutting it close getting to the

bottom before nightfall." Slader crested the rise and started down the other side of the steep incline.

Ten steps forward and suddenly the path gave away, sending Slader plunging down the slope. Kate froze, her mouth hanging open. Then, before she could move or think what to do, the earth beneath her fell away and she went down, too. The force of hitting the ground sent her machete, hanging from her belt, flying into the brush.

Branches clawed at her as she slid down the muddy hillside. Something hit her face, stinging it. She grabbed at a passing bush, but her grip on its wet surface slipped away, her fist clutching a bunch of green leaves instead. She struck a boulder that threw her on her side. Then she rolled downward, her descent increasing. Mud and leaves clogged her mouth. The rumbling of the waterfall grew closer, causing her panic to escalate.

Please, Lord! Don't let me land in the river!

Then with a breath-jarring impact, she came to a stop on a small ledge, no wider than her own body, her arm flung over the side, dangling in space. She quickly pulled it back. She stared upward, rain still falling and hitting her face, cleansing away the mud. She opened her mouth to take in some of the rainwater and try to wash out the grime. Slowly she rose, every square inch of her scratched or aching, and searched the tiny abutment.

Where was Slader? Her panic multiplied. She peered over the ledge.

She sucked in a deep breath. He lay not twenty feet

below her, completely motionless. In the dim light and gray rain she couldn't tell for sure, but it looked like his eyes were closed.

Oh, dear God, please let him be alive. I'm the reason he is here. Please, Father.

She looked around, trying to decide how to get down to him without further hurting herself or sending herself flying over a ledge into space. She could use the rope—that was when she realized she didn't have her backpack. In her plunge down the side of the mountain she'd lost it. Beads of sweat popped out on her face as her panic mushroomed out of control.

"Slader," she shouted down the ravine.

Silence.

Her heart hammered against her rib cage at a maddening tempo while her breathing became shallow gasps. She had to stay calm. Not lose control. Slader needed her.

How could she get to him? She took stock of the area and decided the only way was to ease herself over the ledge and pray she'd find a foothold.

Lord, I know You are with me. Guide me in my descent.

She slipped over the side and felt with her right foot for a place to plant it. Nothing. Then she traded for her left one and found a small jutting of stones. Slowly she made her way down the steep incline, hugging the hillside with every ounce of energy she could muster. Rocks scraped against her. Mud and rain made it difficult to get a firm grip, but she kept going, feeling God's presence with her every inch of the way.

As dark descended and the rain let up, she reached Slader. He lay faceup, not stirring at all. She peeked over the ledge he was on and swallowed hard. Below them the river thundered past. Maybe a thirty-foot drop.

She crawled to Slader, the whole time murmuring, "Father, please let him be alive."

The implications of him being severely hurt or dead was beyond what Kate wanted to consider. When she reached Slader's side, with a trembling hand, she found his pulse at the side of his neck. Then she checked to see if he was breathing. He was.

She collapsed with relief. "Thank You, Lord."

With the light quickly fading, she searched for his injuries and immediately discovered a gash at the back of his head from a rock. Blood covered her fingers as she assessed the extent of the wound. Three inches long. Possibly deep. But the bleeding seemed to have stopped. It was too hard to tell with dusk descending.

What to do? Kate chewed on her bottom lip. Pray.

"Dear Heavenly Father, Slader and I are in quite a bind as You can see. We need Your help to get safely to the river. Slader needs to wake up now. I know the longer he is unconscious, the worse it is. Please, Father, help us. In Jesus Christ, Your Son's name, amen."

Through the pounding pressure in his head, Slader heard the words, "Please, Father, help us. In Jesus Christ, Your Son's name, amen." Everything would be all right, he thought. Kate was here and praying.

He felt the cool touch of her hand as it pushed his hair

from his forehead. Then her fingers wrapped about his, and she began to sing softly about soaring on the wings of an eagle. He listened to her beautiful voice, focusing on the words while trying to ignore the thundering of his heartbeat in his ears that matched the sound of the waterfall below them. For the first time in a long while, he thanked God for being alive. He had to protect Kate.

Kate clung to Slader's hand, willing her strength into him, as she sang, running through a repertorie of songs from church. After the fifth one, she paused, drawing in a deep breath of the moisture-laden air.

"Wake up, Slader. Please."

He stirred. She sat straighter, leaning closer to get a better look despite the darkness creeping over the landscape.

"Slader? Are you awake?"

He groaned, bringing his free hand up to touch his head. "Afraid so."

"Oh, good. You had me worried. Is anything broken?"

"Besides my skull?" He moved his limbs. "Nope, just hurting bad."

"I know you wanted to get to the bottom before nightfall but couldn't you have taken the more traditional way?"

"Funny." He pushed himself to his elbows and slowly examined the area. "This isn't good."

"You think?" Kate barely saw the grin that appeared on Slader's face. Soon she wouldn't be able to see even the hand in front of her when darkness fell completely.

"Touché," he said with a chuckle that stopped abruptly. "I can't laugh. It hurts too much."

"What are we going to do? If you hadn't awakened soon, I confess I didn't have a clue what to do next."

"Sit tight until morning. Not much else we can do. From the sound of it, we're above the waterfall." He felt around. "Where's my backpack?"

"Probably the same place mine is. Either at the bottom or somewhere on the slope above us."

"You don't have yours, either?"

"I'm afraid not."

"We'd better take stock of what we do have besides the clothes on our back." He checked his pockets. "I have a knife, my GPS on my wrist, some matches, a flattened candy bar and that is it. How about you?"

"A lip balm, some mints and a few useless, wet tissues."

"Not promising." He touched his head. "My cap! It's gone, too."

"We're in trouble, aren't we?" She knew the answer but was hoping he would reassure her that they weren't.

"Yep."

She sighed when she heard his answer. "We'll make it."

"Of course we will. I won't let anything happen to you."

"God will take care of us."

She had half suspected he would protest that declaration, but when he didn't, a small ray of hope blossomed in her heart.

Slader sagged against the cliff, bringing his knees up and resting his arms on them.

For a long moment as the dark shadows of night took over, Kate waited for him to say something. When he didn't, she asked, "How's your head?"

Silence.

She shook him gently.

He moaned.

"Slader, you've got to stay awake. You can't sleep tonight."

"I'm tired."

"I am, too, but you can't go to sleep. Not with that head wound." She thought for a moment. How could she keep him awake? "Slader, tell me what you know about the Quentas."

"The Quentas Indians?"

She couldn't see him, but by the tone of his voice she was sure he thought she was crazy. "Yes. After we cross the river tomorrow, we'll be in their territory. I want to know everything you do so I *can* prepare myself."

"I'm not sure you can prepare yourself."

The ominous sound to his words produced a shiver that caused her to hug her arms to her. "I'm quickly realizing that books don't even begin to tell a person what the jungle is really like. So lay it on me. What will we be up against tomorrow?"

"Probably nothing. They'll most likely watch us for a while before deciding what to do about us."

"Will they give us a chance to talk to them?"

For a long moment Slader didn't respond. Kate placed her hand on his arm.

"Kate, I don't know their language. It's different from the other tribes in the area."

She sucked in a deep breath. "That could be a problem."

"Yep. Most definitely."

"How do they hunt? What kind of weapons do they use? How many are there?"

"Whoa, Kate. My head is spinning as it is. I can only answer one question at a time. No one knows for sure how many Quentas there are. The last we heard, at least several hundred."

The idea of several hundred Indians standing in a *large* circle around them with their weapons all pointed at her and Slader took over her mind. "That's a lot. What kind of weapons?"

"The usual I suppose—spears, bows and arrows. I wish I could tell you more. I just don't know much. There are stories circulating about the tribe, but so much of it is probably exaggerated."

"Like what?" Kate relaxed and sat back against the cliff right next to Slader, her arm touching his. He was talking, which meant he wasn't sleeping. That would be her job the whole night, she decided. No matter how much she wished she could sleep herself. She needed Slader and he needed her.

"One is what your brother heard about their extraordinary abilities to heal. No one knows that for sure. Where their village is located is a secret. Even pilots flying over this part of the jungle haven't been able to find any sign of a large village. Of course, they may not live in one large village but several small ones. No one knows."

She heard the weariness in his voice and again touched his arm, trying to convey her support the only way she could. "How are you feeling?"

"Like a few hundred drums are being pounded inside my skull. Other than that, I'm great." He shifted so he faced her. "How about you? That was a long way down."

"Next time, let's not take the shortcut."

His chuckle warmed her. "I'll keep that in mind."

"Tomorrow I'll be sore and bruised, no doubt, but my injuries will not slow us down."

"Speaking of down…we'll still have to find a way to the river, preferably not the way we came to be on this ledge."

"You know the first thing I want when we get back to civilization is a long hot bath. I have mud caked everywhere and this second set of clothes is as bad as the first one."

"Some people pay big money to have mud baths. So where's your appreciation?"

"I think I left it up on the hillside next to my backpack." A loud explosive call sounded over the noise of the waterfall. Kate scooted a little closer to Slader. "What was that?" She didn't dare voice out loud what she thought it was.

"A screaming pia. Don't worry. It's only a bird."

She relaxed some but didn't move away. "What do you want first when you get back to civilization?"

"Hmm. A butter-drenched lobster."

"They have them in Mandras?"

"No, but then I don't consider Mandras civilization."

"Stateside?"

"Too much civilization. Belém is far enough for me."

Kate dragged a deep breath into her lungs and held it for a long moment before asking, "What are you running away from, Slader?" She felt him tense next to her, but she wouldn't take back the question. It was time they got to know each other beyond polite strangers and even the polite part was questionable at times.

"What makes you think I'm running away from anything just because I don't want to go back to the United States?"

"I think a better question is, what are you hiding from?"

A long silence followed her statement, and Kate wondered if he had fallen asleep. She had started to reach for his arm to wake him up when he cut through the quiet with, "Myself."

His solemn tone of voice underscored a shift in their relationship. "Why?" Kate said.

"I killed my wife."

NINE

Slader's words struck Kate like a swift blow to the head, their implication reeling. Her mind went blank while tension claimed every inch of her.

"Or, to put it more accurately," Slader continued in a voice full of self-loathing, "I might as well have killed her. She would be alive today if I hadn't wanted to come to the Amazon to hunt for a lost Amazonian civilization."

"What happened?" she asked, hoping he hadn't felt her go stiff at his declaration. She sensed that this bond forming between them was still so fragile that even a light breeze could break it.

"I met my wife in college. Renee and I were both studying to become archaeologists. I got her interested in South American civilizations and the idea that there was a lost sect of Incas that established an empire within the Amazon that survived much longer than the Incas in Peru after Pizarro and the Spanish destroyed them. After we got married, we scraped together funds for an expedition to seek evidence of this empire."

Slader stopped talking for a long moment, and Kate sensed him slipping into unconsciousness even though she couldn't see him clearly. She quickly laid her hand on his arm, feeling his warmth, and asked, "Did you find it?"

He jerked up. "Find it?"

"The Inca empire."

"No," he replied in a thick, raw voice roughened with emotions she suspected he was trying to control.

"What happened?" For once she hoped he let her glimpse the real man behind the front he presented to the world.

"Renee became pregnant not too long after we started. We decided to stay another month since we hadn't been in the jungle that long, then come back to the States for her to have the baby. We hadn't given up our dream. We intended to return later to the Amazon."

Again, Slader went quiet, but this time Kate knew he was fully awake. The muscles beneath her hand bunched, and he drew in ragged breaths. She waited for him to continue, sensing he was trying to compose himself.

"She developed an infection and died before I could get her back to civilization."

The terse way he'd said *civilization* chilled Kate. She squeezed his arm, hoping to convey her support.

"I buried Renee and my child in the Amazon."

Telling him she was sorry for his loss seemed so inadequate, but the words slipped out anyway.

He grew stiff. "I told her we should go back right away, that the Inca site would be there for us later, but

she wanted to press on for a while longer. It had been
an ordeal just getting to where we were. She was sure
we were so close. I didn't argue with her because
secretly I was glad she wanted to stay. I knew we would
be successful any day and our future would be secured.
A find like that would take years to excavate. Renee and
I would be famous in the academic world with such a
discovery. We would be in demand to write our find, to
lecture about it. The thought was intoxicating…and
my downfall."

The sarcastic twist to his last sentence conveyed his
scorn, all directed at himself. But beneath the contempt,
a thread of hurt laced each word. Kate's heart wrenched
with a need to comfort, something she was sure he
would rebuke. *Father, show me the way to help him.*

"Have you tried to find the Inca site? Is that why you
stayed in Brazil all these years?"

He laughed, a sound filled with such coldness that
Kate shuddered in the warm night air. "I stayed because
Renee is here. That's the least I can do."

"So the Amazon is your prison?"

"My prison? I suppose it is."

"When do you think you'll have done enough
penance for your wife's death? Another five years?
Ten? How long?"

He yanked away from her, putting a few feet
between them, and she suspected if he could, he would
have put more, but the ledge was small and he had to
be precariously close to the edge. Silence pulsated
between them. Tilting her chin, she balled her hands
and prepared to fight him for his soul.

"Is that why you drink?"

"Drink? Alcohol?"

"Yes."

"I haven't had a drop in four years."

Puzzled, Kate remembered the first time she had seen him in the Blue Dolphin with a glass of liquor in front of him. "I don't understand. Back at the bar you had one."

"It's there to remind me of the depths I sank to after Renee's death. I won't go there again. I hardly remember that first year after her death."

Relieved that he hadn't resorted to alcohol to solve his problems, she asked again, "How long do you plan to stay here?"

"I don't know," he practically shouted the words at her, silencing the rain forest around them for a few seconds, the water tumbling over the cliff in the distance the only sound.

The blast of his reply frosted her. She was getting to him, tearing down the barrier he had erected around his heart. Good. It needed to come tumbling down.

"It's none of your—"

"Business?" she asked, cutting into his tirade. "You're right. It isn't. But I've decided to make it my business. After all, you and I are stuck on this ledge all night. For that matter, we are stuck in the middle of a jungle with men after us and possibly an unfriendly tribe of Indians ahead of us. So I think that warrants me getting to know something about you. In exchange, I'll tell you something about me. I think that's fair." Kate knelt with her palms flat on the ground, mud oozing up between her fingers. Never in her life had she been so bold as to say something like that to another. But the words had flown from her mouth as though God himself had spoken them, challenging Slader—for that matter, challenging her.

"Fair? There's nothing fair about this—situation." Slader's voice was now deadly quiet, as though he were gathering his frayed composure about him, shoring up his barrier against her assault.

"Haven't you heard that life isn't fair?" Kate said.

His laughter penetrated the night yet held no humor. "Many times. My life is a good example of that saying."

"Self-pity from you? I'm surprised."

"Not self-pity. I'm just stating the facts, ma'am."

"Zach's all the immediate family I have. My parents and a sister died in a fire when I was in high school, so you aren't the only one who has lost someone special to them." She splayed her muddy hand over heart, momentarily shocked that she had told him something so personal. Only Zach knew her pain. Their loss still wrung her emotionally dry. "They're with the Lord now. I'll see them again one day."

"How do you know you will?"

His question hung in the heavy air between them, his challenge to her. "Because like my faith, theirs was strong."

"But you don't know for a fact what happens to a person after he dies."

"No, that's what faith is all about. Believing in something that isn't necessarily concrete, something you can't put your hands on. Did Renee believe in the Lord?"

"Yes, and it didn't do her any good. She died in my arms with a prayer on her lips. A prayer that went unanswered."

"How do you know it went unanswered?"

"She died! Haven't you been listening to what I said?" His voice rose, drowning out the constant noise from the waterfall.

Kate sensed Slader shifting on the ledge until he was closer to her. "Maybe God's answer was that it was her time to die," Kate said, "that you would be reunited after death. That might not be what you wanted, but that doesn't mean it wasn't best for Renee."

The sound of his snort centered her attention on Slader. Even though it was too dark to see him fully, she could picture the wry slant to his mouth, the derision in his expression.

"What would it take to shake that faith of yours? Not finding Zach?"

"If the Lord wants Zach, I won't stand in His way. But I don't think that is what the Lord has planned for my brother. We will find him."

"And how do you know that?"

"In here." She clenched her hand over her heart. "God is with us. We will make it. I just know it."

"Some people would call you a fool to believe so blindly."

"We've made it this far. We'll make it the rest of the way."

In the dim light of the half moon, no longer covered

by clouds, Kate observed him touching the back of his head although she still couldn't see his expression.

"We're going to make it, but I didn't necessarily say in what kind of condition." She forced a lightness into her voice, wanting not to consider the gravity of the situation for a little while.

"You tell me this now when my head's pounding and every part of me hurts."

"Well, look on the bright side. We're nearly to the bottom of the hill and it didn't take long."

He laughed, a robust sound that competed with the other noises in the jungle. "For future reference, I think the more traditional way is better. Probably wouldn't hurt as much."

"I'll keep that in mind." She eased herself back against the rock face at the same time he settled next to her, their arms touching. "Have you climbed many hills?" she asked, hoping he would reveal a little more about himself. There were still a few hours to dawn, and she was afraid to have him go to sleep. She was afraid to go to sleep herself. One false move and either one of them could continue the journey to the bottom of the hill—swiftly, dangerously.

"A few. How about you? As I seem to recall, there aren't that many hills in Oklahoma."

She smiled at the way he had turned the conversation around and focused it on her. She had learned more about him tonight than he had probably ever told anyone in a long time, except Renee. "There are a few. Oklahoma isn't totally flat, at least not the eastern half of the state. How about where you're from? Are there many hills?"

"I think we're stuck on one right now."

She gritted her teeth. He would have been the perfect spy. No one would have gotten a thing out of him unless he wanted them to know it. "I meant when you lived in the United States."

"I know what you meant. You're bound and determined to have my life history."

She remained quiet.

He sighed. "Okay. Here goes. It's a short life history so it won't eat up much time. I was born in Tennessee, not the mountain part, but Memphis. My father wasn't around when I was growing up. My mother worked all the time to feed and clothe me and my sister. My childhood wasn't anything I would want to write about. I went into the service so I could go to college on the government's tab. I served my time, then went to the University of Arizona where I eventually got my doctorate in archaeology before moving to Texas. End of story."

Hardly the end of the story, Kate thought, rolling her head around on her shoulders. She knew the discussion of the relevant parts of his life was over. She would have to be satisfied with what she had discovered. "Very good. And the world as we know it did not come to an end with that revelation."

"Ouch. I think my sarcasm is rubbing off on you. Okay. It's your turn. What's your life story?"

"Mine is even shorter than yours. I grew up in Red Creek and that is the only place I've lived. Zach is all the family I have left, except a grandfather. I am the secretary at my church. End of story."

"I doubt that. How old were you when your parents and sister died?"

She'd hoped he hadn't latched on to that bit of her story. His question produced buried emotions that rose into her throat and lumped together. She swallowed hard and tried to form an answer. No words would come to mind.

"Kate?" Slader took her hands and cupped them between his, facing her.

The gesture released the dam on her tears, and they flowed down her cheeks. She cleared her throat and squeaked out, "Seventeen."

His arm slid around her, and he pulled her close to him.

Laying her head on his shoulder, she said in a stronger voice, "Tess was only fifteen and that afternoon we'd had a huge fight because she was taking my clothes and wearing them to school. She hadn't bothered to return them and I found several items in her room on her floor. There was a particular piece of clothing that I wanted to take on the church retreat Zach and I were going on for the weekend. I wanted to look extra nice for a boy I had a crush on. The shirt was dirty and wrinkled. I yelled at her and she yelled at me." Tears jammed Kate's throat, locking in her words. She could still see in her mind's eye the scene as if it had happened yesterday. Every line of her body had spoken her anger at Tess down to the balled hands at her sides.

Slader squeezed her closer. "What happened?"

His gentle tone urged her to release the torment she

hadn't expressed to another soul, not even her twin. "I stormed out of her room, telling Tess I wished I didn't have a little sister. That night a fire consumed our house and my family. I no longer had a little sister." Tears streamed down her face and for the first time she truly cried for her loss. Guilt had stopped her for years—a guilt she had kept pushing out of her conscious mind because she hadn't wanted to deal with it.

"And you think God granted you your wish?"

She nodded, then realized he might not see her action and said, "Yes—I mean, no. God isn't like that, but at seventeen I thought that."

"That you were the reason your parents and sister died?"

"Yes. Later I realized how much I needed the Lord's love and forgiveness. He's what has sustained me during the tough times."

He took her chin and brought her face around so he could look her in the eye, even though it was too dark to see much. "Believe me, you weren't responsible." He wiped away the tears that continued to fall.

"There's a part of me that realizes that, but I never got to ask Tess for her forgiveness. I never got to right what I said to her the last time I saw her. Do you understand now why it is so important for me to find Zach? I can't lose another sibling. Zach's all I have."

He framed her face with his large hands. "Yes, but what if he isn't alive? Are you prepared for that?"

"He is alive."

His long sigh brushed against her lips right before his mouth settled on hers, his searing kiss a total shock.

When he pulled back, Kate wanted to take his face between her hands and demand another kiss. His touch fell away, and he put some distance between them.

"I shouldn't have done that."

"Why did you?" Kate missed the feel of his mouth on hers, the comfort of his arms around her. For one brief moment the loneliness had been held at bay in his embrace.

"It seemed the right thing to do at the time." He adjusted himself against the rock face, his arms resting on his raised knees. "We need to discuss our next move."

"What next move?" *Another kiss?* Kate wondered, not at all appalled at the idea.

"Should we go forward into the unknown or go back to Mandras?"

"We can't go back!"

"Kate, we don't have anything but the clothes we are wearing. The jungle isn't the lush environment everyone thinks it is. It's hard to make it with nothing but our bare hands."

"You have a knife."

"That won't cut down very much."

"What about the men after us?"

"That's a bit of a problem, but we can probably skirt around them. It's just you and me and no supplies. Kate, I made a promise to myself long ago that I would not bury another woman out here in the jungle. I won't break that promise to myself. I won't."

"And, being a woman, I am grateful for that promise, but I made a promise to myself. I will find Zach."

"So this is a Mexican standoff?"

"Not exactly. Going back could be more dangerous than going forward. You don't know otherwise. But if I go back, I won't find Zach. That's a definite."

He barked a laugh. "You are one stubborn woman."

"Yes, sadly I am. I'm working on that. And my lack of patience."

"You're gonna have to compromise on this. I'll go forward for a few more days. If we don't find your brother, then we're going back to Mandras. Deal?"

Kate chewed her bottom lip, still remembering Slader's kiss.

"Kate, deal?"

"Okay. I guess I don't have a choice in the matter."

"No, you don't, because I will bring you back to Mandras over my shoulder if I have to."

The picture of Slader carrying her slung over his shoulder popped into her mind, and she chuckled. "That's an awfully long trek and I'm not what you would call slender."

"Where there's a will, there's a way."

The words were said in jest, but Kate heard the determination behind them and knew he would do exactly what he had threatened if she balked at going back to Mandras in a few days. *Lord, I only have a short time to find Zach. Please point us in the right direction.*

"What about our backpacks? Do you think we might be able to find them?"

"It's possible they are at the bottom of this hill. It's also possible they are somewhere along the path we took down the hill."

"I think we should search for them." Kate stared at the sky growing light with streaks of orange and yellow woven through the dark.

"You're right."

"I am? This is a first, you admitting I am right."

"Funny," he said with a chuckle.

Rubbing at her arm, she said, "Mud baths are highly overrated. I for one can't wait to wash this mud off me."

"You'll get your chance. Below we'll have to swim across the river to get to the other side."

"Swim?"

"You can, can't you?"

"Yes, but what about the piranhas?"

"They aren't as bad as they are made out to be. Usually they don't attack people."

"*Usually* is the operative word here."

"You'll be all right."

"Promise?"

"Yes."

Somehow she felt as though he would protect her against anything that might attack her in the water, so she refused to think anymore about what might lurk there.

"We'll wait until it's totally light then head out," he said, stretching each leg as if testing them to make sure they worked after his spill down the hill.

Then Slader turned his head and searched the area, his strong features highlighted by the gray shadows of dawn. Kate hugged her legs to her chest and rested her head on her knees, watching him. With lightning quickness, his attention returned to her before she had a chance to close her eyes. His gaze ensnared hers and for a long moment she felt trapped by his look.

The corner of his mouth slanted upward, and he said, "You should get a little rest. I promise not to go to sleep so you won't have to worry about me losing consciousness."

"I'm tired, but I can't sleep now. Besides, it won't be long before it's fully light."

"True."

His gaze continued to drill into hers. "I look a mess."

He reached out and plucked a leaf from her wild mane. "I like your hair down."

The air between them electrified. She sat up, her tongue slipping across her dry, cracked lips. Staring at him, she wanted to tell him she liked everything about him, but she didn't say a word. Even with his face scratched and two days' growth of a beard, he looked wonderful to her eyes.

"You shouldn't wear your hair up." He glanced away as though suddenly embarrassed and slowly rose on the small ledge, holding his hand out for her to take.

She slid hers into his grasp, and he pulled her up to stand beside him. Below them, through the gray mist that shrouded the jungle, ran a river with a small waterfall no more than twenty-five feet upstream. A blanket of green covered the landscape for miles with little interruption except for an occasional tree that thrust itself high above the others around it. A colorful bird with yellow and green feathers flew close and landed on a branch not far from them. Its thrilling song filled the early morning air.

Kate turned to say something to Slader at the same moment he turned toward her. There were only inches between them.

He smoothed a stray strand of her hair behind her ear and cupped the back of her neck. "You're not as plain looking as you want people to believe, Kate. Why do you hide behind unflattering clothes and a 'do not approach' attitude?"

She straightened, shrugging away from his touch and trying to muster anger at his question. But she couldn't. His question bored into her, demanding she take a good hard look at her life. The past night had stirred memories she hadn't allowed herself to think about in a long while. "Because that is who I am," she finally answered, no conviction behind her words.

He brought his arms to his side, but sympathy was in his eyes. "Maybe you aren't the only one serving penance for a past action."

She took a step back, careful not to go too far. "What do you mean?" There was more strength in her voice this time.

"I mean your guilt over your sister's death. You yelled at her for wearing a shirt you had wanted to wear to impress a guy. Now you go out of your way to dress in a way that is certain not to attract a guy."

"There's nothing wrong with how I dress."

"So you like the school-marm-in-mourning look?"

She opened her mouth to deny his words but couldn't. She snapped it closed.

Slader stepped into her personal space. She thought about moving away but was trapped by the narrowness of the ledge. She brought her hands up to push him back. Capturing them, he held them against his chest. "In Red Creek, do you date?"

"It's none of your business."

"As you told me earlier, I'm making it my business. Do you date, Kate?"

The intensity of his question battered her defenses. "No. I'm very busy and don't have much time for dating."

"Doing what?"

"Working." She threw her shoulders back. "Volunteering. Reading. Gardening and…" She couldn't think of anything else she really did with her time.

"And doing a fine job of running away from life."

"I do not. I am quite involved in my church and I serve on several committees. I have a lot of friends."

"Any of them male?"

The space between them shrunk even more. Her breathing became shallow, raspy. "Sure. There's the reverend at our church and Mr. Benson next door."

"Any males between the ages of thirty and forty-five?"

She thought for a moment, then slowly shook her head.

"My point exactly. Ever since your sister's death you have hidden yourself from the opposite sex. You think that will make up for what you wished that day you fought with Tess."

Anger took hold of her finally. "And from experience you know that it doesn't work—hiding that is. Life has a way of finding you."

For one split second her anger ruled, then suddenly it melted away, leaving her clinging to him for support. His hand fisted in her thick, wild hair and held her still while his mouth claimed hers in a kiss not anything like the gentle, brief one a few hours before. This one went straight to her heart. Legs weak, she dug her fingernails into his shoulders while his mouth possessed hers.

When he finally moved back, his dark, dark gaze pierced her. "We'd better get moving. We have a long way to go today and we need to find at least one of our backpacks and maybe one of the machetes. I released mine when I knew I was going to tumble down the hill. What happened to yours?"

"Mine released itself when I went tumbling down the hill. Everything happened so fast, I doubt I would have thought to untie it."

He gave her an odd look. "Someone's watching out for you."

"God is."

"Perhaps you're right."

"I know I am."

He turned away and stared down the hill, then up the way they had come. "I don't see anything. Do you remember where you were when you lost your backpack?"

"I don't remember much except branches clawing me and green whirling by."

He ran his hand through his hair. "Neither do I."

Kate eased herself to the ledge and looked over into the dense jungle below. Squinting as though that would make a difference, she scanned the area. Something blue caught her attention. A bird? Her backpack was blue. "Look. What do you think that is?"

Slader peered at the place she pointed at. "That might be your backpack. There's only one way to find out."

"Go down?"

"Yes, we go down, preferably at a more controlled rate."

Kate stood at the edge of the river fifty yards down from the small waterfall, staring at the water that flowed by at a more sedate pace than she had imagined. She had to swim across. What choice did she have? Across the river was where Zach was. Her crash course in learning to swim before coming to the Amazon suddenly didn't seem long enough for her to get herself to the other side.

"Kate, what aren't you telling me?" Slader moved in front of her, blocking her view of the river.

"Until a few weeks ago I didn't swim at all. When I decided I had to search for my brother myself, I took some lessons from a friend."

"You can't swim?"

"I can swim. I'm just not sure how good I am at it."

"Lady, that explains why you almost drowned a few days ago."

She bristled at his use of the word *lady* as though their time on the ledge had counted for nothing when in her heart she would never forget how close she had felt to him. "*Mr.* Slader, I will swim across that river and I will do it without any help from you." She lifted her chin and glared at him.

His laughter echoed through the jungle. "I can always count on your stubborn streak, *Kate*. If it will make you feel any better, you shouldn't have to swim much. This is the end of the dry season when the water is at its lowest even with the rain that has fallen in the past twenty-four hours." He gestured at the river. "See all those sandbars. During the rainy season there aren't any. Are you ready?"

She nodded, gulping down the fear that threatened to surface as she stepped closer to the river. The water all of a sudden seemed to be rushing by her at a quick pace. The rumble of the waterfall masked the thundering heartbeat that had lodged in her throat.

"I'll take that." Slader pried her fingers loose from around the straps of her backpack that they had blessedly found intact at the bottom of the hill. He started for the water.

"Wait! I should see to your head wound first."

He peered over his shoulder. "Let's get across the river, then you can play nurse."

"But—"

"Kate!"

She tried to draw in a fortifying breath, but only managed to fill her lungs a little. Inhaling again, deeper this time, she trailed him into the river, keeping her focus trained on the other side.

"I'll go first. I want you right behind me to the side so I can keep an eye on you." He waded farther out until the water was up past his waist. "Ready."

"Sure," she said in a shaky whisper that she was certain he hadn't heard over the noise of the waterfall.

He plunged in, swimming with the backpack held up out of the water, even though it was waterproof.

God is with me, she thought, her fear subsiding. She followed suit, doing something that was a cross between the crawl and the dog paddle. She wouldn't earn points on technique today, but she was determined to get to the other side. Fighting the current threw her against Slader on a couple of occasions as she tried to keep pace with him. Her lungs burned with the effort.

Only a few more feet, she thought and shifted her focus to the side where a sandbar, littered with several logs, came up out of the water. One moved. A caiman, at least six feet long and dark brown, rose up on its short legs, in the middle of the sandbar. It fixed its stare on them, sizing them up for a snack. The creature took a few steps toward the river.

Kate screamed, "Get out of the water," and propelled herself as fast as she could toward the curtain of green.

She heard the splash behind her and to the left where the sandbar was, but she didn't dare take her eyes off her destination, a tree trunk she thought she could climb near the bank. Slader scrambled out of the river a shade ahead of her, then turned and offered her his hand. He yanked her up and out of the water, shoving her toward the large tree a few feet away. She clambered its rough trunk, pulling herself up using the ladderlike branches to climb it.

Below them, the caiman paused at the river's edge, his dark eyes taking them both in as they clung to the tree for dear life. Slader's chest rose and fell as rapidly as hers did. Slader never looked away from the beast until the animal decided they weren't going to be his latest dinner. He sank into the murky water and vanished.

With the caiman's disappearance Kate swiped her forearm across her brow and released a long breath between pursed lips. "At least I made it."

Slader's chuckles peppered the air. "We're even. That's the second time you've come to my rescue. For such a novice, Kate, you're a remarkable woman, especially since you can't swim worth a—" he paused, searching for the right words, "plugged nickel."

She beamed with his praise. "That caiman probably uses that ploy on wayward animals all the time. He certainly is one tricky creature, lying in wait among the logs."

"He could be a she."

She laughed. "True. How long do you think we should stay up here?"

Slader studied the river, especially where the caiman had sunk below the water. "I think it's probably looking for easier prey. I'll go down first."

"I'll keep an eye out, just in case our friend decides to return."

Slader's gaze caught hers and for a moment she thought she saw surprise in his eyes, as though he wasn't used to someone looking out for him. That thought pricked her heart. She had grown up in a loving, warm family, but she didn't think Slader had. His marriage to Renee had been his chance at a family and it had been snatched away from him before he had really experienced what a family meant.

"It's safe, Kate. Come on." He reached up to help her scale down the trunk.

The rough bark scraped her skin, especially her palms, as she descended. She turned her face and the bark cut into her cheek. By the time she landed with both feet on the wet ground, she felt battered and bruised but alive. She whirled around, exhilarated by her successful swim and the fact she had been the one to first spot the caiman.

Slader's intense look stole her words. As if in slow motion, he touched her cheek in a featherlight caress that curled her toes.

"You're hurt. Let's get away from the river and see to your injury."

The mesmerizing cadence of his voice melted her as if she were a block of ice in a desert. "Only after I fix your head. Remember you promised I could."

With a smile he grabbed the backpack he had dropped in his mad dash up the tree and slung it over his shoulder. "You don't forget a thing, do you?"

"Nope. I'm glad you've figured that out."

He scanned the dense undergrowth. "This isn't going to be easy since we couldn't find either one of the machetes. I'll go first and try to make a path for you."

Her heart swelled at the protective ring to his words. "You know the good thing about swimming that river is that we're no longer muddy from head to toe."

"No, we are wet instead."

"Isn't that the usual mode here in the jungle, some form of wetness?"

"Yeah, that's why clothes don't last long. They fall apart."

"Well, let's hope our clothes last a little bit longer."

Two hours later Slader stopped in a section of the rain forest that was relatively clear of underbrush and shaded by the tall trees that formed the green canopy above them. Sitting on a log that was beginning to decompose, Kate rummaged through her backpack to find the first-aid kit and extra bottle of alcohol she had brought.

"Ready," she said, looking up. When she realized Slader wasn't in front of her, she shot to her feet and spun around. Relief sagged her shoulders as she spied him several yards away, cutting down some palm nuts with his Swiss army knife.

"Lunch and breakfast," he announced when he had succeeded in his task.

"Let's don't mention food. I'm way past hungry. Thankfully we have my canteen and the pills to treat the water." She motioned him to her.

Again she sat on the log while he settled on the ground in front of her so she could clean the back of his head. "This will sting." She poured some of the alcohol into his wound.

Slader flinched but remained seated. "Will I live?"

"Afraid so. It's not too deep or long." She finished cleansing the wound, then started to put everything back into her pack.

"Hold it. It's my turn to tend to your injuries. I've noticed your palms are cut up, too," he said, rising.

"I can take care of them."

"And your face." He took the kit from her and removed the cotton pads and the alcohol. "It's important to keep our sores and wounds as clean as possible. Infections are—" His voice came to abrupt halt.

Standing, Kate placed her hands over his. She remembered what had killed Renee—an infection. The beating of her heart slowed to a painful throb as she watched him wrestle with his memories.

"Slader, I'm so sorry for what happened to your wife, but it was not your fault. You've got to believe that. It was no one's fault. You two made a choice together. Things happen that we have no control over. This was one of them. You need to forgive yourself for living when she didn't."

He pulled his hands free. "What I need to do is clean up your wounds."

"Slader—"

"Don't, Kate. This isn't the time nor the place to discuss my past."

"But I hate to see—"

"You have your own demons to take care of, Kate."

His words, said in anger, found their mark. Kate stepped back, determined to tend to her own cuts. She reached for the kit. Slader wouldn't give it to her, a determined expression on his face.

"Let me know when you're ready," he said in a cold voice.

She brought her hands up to hug her shivering body. He fumbled with the alcohol, finally managing to open the plastic bottle and drenching the cotton pad. She stood her ground, her gaze burrowing into him as he patted her cheek in a gentle touch that contradicted his expression.

When he was satisfied, he said, "Let me see your hands."

She held one out, upset that her fingers shook as he grasped them. He doused the cuts on her palms with alcohol, the burning sensation momentarily focusing her attention away from Slader. He lifted first one hand then the other and blew on her stinging flesh. The warmth of his breath rivaled the chill created by the quickly evaporating alcohol.

Finished, he put the first-aid kit away, then shrugged into the backpack. He turned toward her and their gazes locked. Not a word was spoken. The only sounds were the chattering noises from a band of monkeys above them and the clicking of various insects.

"I'm sorry, Kate," Slader finally said.

She knew that he didn't apologize often, and the fact that he had was a step forward in the precarious relationship developing between them. Because ever since the night before, on the ledge, there was a bond between them that was growing stronger with each step deeper into the jungle. It should have frightened her, and back in Red Creek it would have. But right now it didn't.

A crashing sound riveted their attention and through the trees came a herd of stampeding peccaries. Paralyzed, Kate tried to count the hordes of pigs, squealing as they headed toward them.

"Run!" Slader grabbed her hand and tugged her into action.

She hurried with him as the squeals grew louder. One peccary shot past them. Slader threw Kate behind a large tree, plastering her against its bark with his body as her only protection.

The frenzy of noise intensified. The pounding of her heart kept pace with the pigs that had invaded the jungle around them. With the deafening sound in her ears, she prayed to the Lord to spare them and if possible, to leave one behind for their dinner.

She felt Slader's heart beat rapidly against her back, his warm breath washing over her neck and sending tingles down her spine. A few seconds before, she had been frightened for their safety, but suddenly a calm descended and she let her fear go. With God and Slader on her side, nothing was going to harm her. *Thank You, Lord, for sending me Slader.*

As quickly as the peccary herd had descended on them, it was gone, their loud squealing still audible in the distance. Slader moved away from the large tree trunk that had protected them from the wild pigs gone crazy.

He breathed deeply. "That was close. I knew a guy last year who was killed in one of those stampedes by a herd of peccaries. Something must have frightened them. Maybe a jaguar."

Kate glanced past Slader's shoulder and her world came to a standstill. "I don't think it was a jaguar."

TEN

Slader and Kate were surrounded by men no more than five feet tall, all painted red, black and white with long spears raised and pointed at them. Kate automatically took a step toward Slader, her breath trapped in her lungs until they burned. These Indians had to belong to the Quentas tribe. This was their territory, and she and Slader had trespassed, something the warriors didn't like, if their fierce expressions were any indication.

"What do we do?" Kate whispered, noting one particular Indian dressed with more brightly colored feathers than the others. Was he the leader?

"Good question," Slader said.

Just as Slader answered her, the group of Indians ran toward them, spears still pointed at them. Kate froze.

Lord, if this is my time, so be it, but please—

The men came to an abrupt stop a few feet from her and Slader. The Quentas stabbed their spears in the air while yelling at them.

Dear Heavenly Father, Slader is here because of me.

I should have let him turn back. Please protect him. The prayer had barely formed in her mind when Slader stepped in front of her and shielded her with his body, using the tree trunk to cover her back.

Over the yelling, Slader spoke in a language she couldn't understand and she didn't think was Portuguese or Spanish but most likely one of the Indian dialects he knew. Looking at the sea of men crowding in on them, Kate knew there was no way she and Slader could fight their way out of this predicament even if they'd had their machetes, which they didn't. Was this what Zach had been greeted with when he'd made contact?

But before any doubts could manifest themselves in her mind, the Indians became suddenly quiet and a strong baritone voice sounded from behind them in a strange language. She would know that voice anywhere. Zach.

Elation sent her flying forward, but Slader grabbed her before she headed into the mob of warriors. "Zach!"

"I should have known you would come looking for me, Kate."

The Indians parted, and she saw her twin brother for the first time in months. Shrugging off Slader's hand, she shouted her joy and rushed forward, throwing herself into his arms. "I *knew* you were alive! You're too mean to die." *Thank You, Lord!*

"Hey, is that any kind of greeting after I saved your pretty little neck?" Zach laughed.

"What's going on, Zach?" Kate scanned the Indians with spears still pointed at them.

"I've known you were coming for several days—or rather, they did." He nodded toward the crowd about them. "They've been tracking your movements. This is their way of greeting someone special to me."

"What did you do to make them so mad?"

"Nothing, sis. That demonstration was a good welcome." Zach smiled.

"I'd hate to see a bad one."

"You wouldn't. You'd be dead," Zach gestured toward one of the spears. "They would be dipped in poison."

Kate shuddered. "A few minutes ago I thought we were dead." As she said *we,* she turned toward Slader and motioned him to her. "I want to introduce you to my guide, Slader."

Slader sauntered toward Kate and Zach, keeping a wary eye on the Indians staring at him. "I take it you're Zach." He shook her brother's outstretched hand.

The man whom Kate was sure was the chief said something to Zach. Her brother replied, then turned to them. "We came to get you since it appears you've lost your supplies. They'll be setting a fast pace back to their village. We're pretty far from it. We can talk more when we get there."

"Why are we going back to their village?" Kate asked, not sure about the Quentas Indians even if they had taken her brother in. Fierce expressions still graced their faces, she realized, partially due to the paint they wore, but still, the effect caused her to pause.

"Sis, you're going because they have asked you to. They have befriended me, and I wouldn't turn down their hospitality if I were you. It isn't extended often."

"And that's supposed to reassure me?"

This time Slader laughed. "I'm so glad it isn't just me who brings out that sharp, inquisitive tongue of hers."

"Try being her brother and growing up with her."

"My condolences."

"You two," Kate said with her hands on her hips. "I'm standing right here, listening to every word."

"She always stuck her nose in my business." Zach fell into step, leading the way.

"And you should be glad I did. I found you when no one else could."

Zach threw her a glance over his shoulder. "It looks like *we* found you. Besides, I wasn't lost. I knew where I was. I figured the authorities would have given up the search after a month."

"Then why didn't you return to Mandras?" Kate asked, unable to keep her exasperation from her voice.

Zach waved his hand in the air, dismissing the question. "Can't answer right now, sis. We'll talk later and I'll explain everything."

"But I've come…" Her words faded as the Indians set a hard pace through the rain forest, making it impossible to talk because she was trying to keep up and not fall flat on her face.

The Quentas moved at a trot with one foot planted directly in front of the other, not one wasted motion, on a narrow path through the now thick vegetation. Even as resolved as she was, Kate found herself lagging farther behind the main body of Indians. Sweat flowed off her as though it were raining again and her breathing quickly became labored. She peered behind her at Slader who was trying his best not to step on her heels.

She dug into her well of determination and came up dry. *Lord, I'm not going to make it. Help me.*

Fifteen minutes later, Slader called out to Zach, "Can they slow the pace any? After my tumble down that hill, I'm not in the best of condition."

Bless the man, Kate thought, chancing a look at him, worry about him nibbling at her. He wasn't sweating much and his breathing was normal. He seemed all right. His motive dawned on her at the same time he winked at her. She twisted back around and nearly collided into her brother's back.

Zach grabbed her to steady her while Slader did, too. Sandwiched between the two men, she saw the Quentas stopped on the path ahead, crowding in on them.

One said something to Zach who answered him, then her brother faced her. "It'll be dark when we get to the village, but they will slow down for you…two." He looked from Kate to Slader, who quirked a brow, something shared silently between Slader and Zach.

No doubt some kind of male bonding, Kate thought irritably.

The Indians resumed their trek through the rain forest, but at least this time it was at a fast walk. Remembering the silent exchange between Slader and Zach, Kate bolstered her determination not to ask for a single other thing.

Two hours later, the Quentas stopped for a brief

respite, which Kate knew was because of her. After looking back at her, Zach had said something to the man in front of him. Not ten minutes had passed before they had come to a river. Several warriors went into the jungle and brought back a strange-looking vine, which they sliced and gave to Kate and Slader.

"Drink from it, Kate." Zach took a vine from an Indian. "It'll help you. I'm not sure how, but it has a restorative power that I want to explore more thoroughly in a lab."

"I'm ready to try anything. I'm wiped. A wet noodle has more strength than I do." She tipped the vine, and a clear liquid flowed into her mouth. Its metallic taste was different but not unpleasant.

After draining the liquid in her vine, a warrior motioned them toward the water. Hidden in the underbrush by the river's edge were four canoes. Kate and Slader were instructed to get into one while Zach settled into another.

Kate knew it was still midafternoon when they headed out onto the narrow river, but the thick canopy overhead blocked most of the sunlight, creating an eerie darkness. The sounds coming from the jungle— a few she hadn't heard before—heightened her fear and feeling of total isolation. One series of five sharp barks sent her nearly to her feet in the canoe. Slader's hand on her shoulder stopped her.

"It's just a *cora* rat, Kate. Nothing to worry about."

She forced herself to relax, beginning to feel the restorative effects of the strange liquid from the vine. At least now she could sit straight in the canoe and keep her head and shoulders from sagging forward in exhaustion.

Kate looked back at Slader. "This river is completely hidden from the air. I feel like we are traveling in a tunnel of trees."

"We are. I've heard of this river for years, but I've never known anyone who has been on it. Rest, Kate, I have a feeling we still have a bit of walking to do."

When the Indians rowed toward shore an hour later, Slader's prediction came true. Kate climbed from the canoe with Slader right behind her. Zach stood on the bank waiting for them, then they followed the Quentas into the thick rain forest.

As the jungle grew dark with the approach of night, Kate wanted to collapse in the middle of the narrow path. The only thing that kept her going was the danger such a move would put her in. Somehow she managed to place one foot in front of the other.

When the lead warrior stopped at the base of a cliff, Kate scanned the area, dense with undergrowth, and wondered where in the world the village was. It would be completely dark in fifteen minutes. Then a Quentas disappeared into the side of the cliff. Kate squinted, trying to see more clearly. Under a crag there appeared to be a narrow hole in the rocks.

"We go up now," Zach said, motioning toward that hole.

"How?" Kate thought of the darkness and didn't understand.

"The village is at the top of this cliff. There's a pathway through the mountain to the village."

Suddenly a flare of light lit the opening in the cliff.

"They're an amazing people, but even they can't see in the dark." Zach took Kate's hand to help her toward the entrance.

"I can see why these Indians have been so isolated," Slader said behind Kate.

As the dank walls of the cave closed in on Kate, her heart rate accelerated and even more sweat drenched her body.

"How long?" she managed to ask her brother in a raspy whisper.

He paused and turned toward her. "I forgot about your claustrophobia. I'm sorry, Kate. This is the only way up and it takes about an hour. At some places it's a steep climb."

"I'll make it." And somehow she would. *Lord, I need Your help. I know my fear is irrational. Nothing will happen to me. But still I'm scared. Please be with me each step of the way.*

As she climbed, she was aware of three things. Zach was in front of her carrying one of the torches, setting an easy pace. Slader was behind her, helping her when the rocks and path were steep and difficult. God was inside her, giving her the strength she needed to traverse the cave system, to not care that she was inside a mountain where tons of heavy rocks could come crashing down on her.

When she emerged from the passageway into the open, she took her first decent breath since their trek through the cave had started. She drew in gulps of the oxygen-rich air, heavy with the scent of vegetation. In the distance she saw lights from several fires. The village, beneath towering trees, was completely hidden from above.

Thank You, God, for getting us this far safely. Thank You for giving me Zach back. And again thank You for bringing Slader into my life, even if it's only for a short time.

On the village's outskirts she fell to her knees, her shoulders drooping forward, so exhausted she didn't think she could go another step. She buried her face in her hands and sank to the ground. Someone put a hand on her shoulder, then knelt next to her. She didn't have the energy even to see who it was.

"Kate?"

Slader's voice penetrated her weary mind with his concern.

"I'm okay," she murmured, but her voice belied her words.

"Sure you are, but I'm going to help you anyway."

She started to protest his assistance, then decided a little help into the village was all right. He bore most of her weight as she came to her feet with his arm now around her shoulders. Leaning against him, she stepped forward, but the world tilted and faded out of focus.

Before she realized what he was doing, he swung her up into his arms and strode toward the center of the village. She should have objected, but the effort to form the words was too great. Instead, she wilted like a water-deprived plant against him, her head cushioned on his shoulder.

For a moment she closed her eyes and listened to the

sounds of the village. Soft murmurs, a baby's crying punctuated the noises of the jungle beyond. Slader's familiar scent dominated the smells that assailed her— smoke, roasting meat, decomposing vegetation.

When she opened her eyes again, she found herself in a dimly lit, large, oblong hut. A hole cut into its high ceiling allowed the smoke from the many fires to escape. Around the center were numerous hammocks slung from poles that held the structure up. Several Indian women, all staring at them, fanned the air with large palm fronds.

"Put her there," Zach said, indicating a hammock not far from the doorway.

"That's okay. I don't want to take someone's bed." She straightened, aware that the whole hut full of people was now watching them.

"It's my bed and you can have it," Zach said. "Slader and I will sleep on the ground."

"Is that safe?" she asked, remembering the stories of what crawled on that ground.

"Yes, sis. We'll be fine."

"Then I'm not going to argue with you because I'm dead tired and all I want to do is sleep."

"That's a first," Zach said with a laugh. "All you've ever done is argue with me."

"And believe me, I will first thing tomorrow morning," she said with a smile. "Then you have some explaining to do."

Slader lay her in the hammock, steadying it before stepping back. For some strange reason, she wanted to grab his arm and hold him next to her. Everything around her was so different. Yes, she had read books about the Amazon, but nothing had prepared her for the Indians staring at her or their lifestyle so obviously dissimilar from hers. She didn't even wear makeup, yet they were covered with paints and designs.

"Will you be all right?" Slader whispered, hovering over her.

She did reach out and take his hand, the concern in his expression unraveling her faster than anything else that had happened to her that day. She wanted to ask him the same thing, especially after all he had shared with her up on the hillside. Instead, she squeezed his hand and nodded. "I'm tough. Nothing much gets me down for long."

His chuckle filled the space between them. "I can attest to that. I will tell you I'm not comfortable staying here, not with all I've heard about the Quentas."

Kate leaned around Slader and caught sight of her brother who was speaking with an elder. "Zach seems to have settled right in."

"Yeah, well, we need to convince him to leave immediately. There have been cases where the Quentas have turned on their guests." He rubbed his hand along the back of his neck.

"Do you have that itch again?"

"Not exactly. Just an uncomfortable feeling that we don't belong here." He smiled, the look in his eyes totally focused on her. "I'm sure everything is all right. You get some rest and we'll talk in the morning." He backed away.

Now how in the world, Lord, am I supposed to get

any rest with those parting words? Please protect us
and be with us. Guide us safely back to Mandras. And
oh, yeah, keep us safe from Slick and his cohorts. Amen.

Slader couldn't sleep. He should be dead tired and
his body was. But his mind couldn't rest. He didn't like
being smack-dab in the middle of a bunch of Indians
who he had last heard were hostile to anyone who
came into their territory. And they were definitely in
the middle of their territory, Slader thought, taking in
his surroundings in the large hut with the Quentas tribe
all around them sleeping.

A snore from a nearby Indian penetrated the silence
of the hut. Slader smiled to himself. So far, the Quentas
didn't seem so warlike.

"You're worried, aren't you?" Zach settled next to
him on a grass mat that would serve as a bed.

"Are you aware that some men are following Kate and
me? They didn't want Kate to find you. You're in danger."

Zach blew out an exasperated breath. "I knew there
were others in the area. Wasn't sure why."

"A man named Slick assaulted Kate in Mandras."

"Was she hurt?" Zach fisted his hands, his features
set in a scowl.

"No, I stopped him before he could do any real
harm. Someone, possibly Slick, also trashed her hotel
room. Slick followed us with three other men up the
river and I'm sure they are waiting for us, no doubt to
kill us. Our two porters skipped out on us. I'm not sure
if it was because of the men after us or the fact we were
nearing the Quentas territory."

"Probably a little of both. I had a hard time getting any porters for my expedition and two ran off four days in."

Slader pulled his legs up, resting his arms on his knees. "So what happened? When they couldn't find you, everyone except Kate thought you were dead."

"We were ambushed and I was left for dead. If it hadn't been for the Quentas, I would be dead right now. I had two other scientists with me. They didn't survive. I managed to crawl into the underbrush and camouflage myself. Even then, if it hadn't been for the arrival of the Quentas warriors, I would have been found and finished off."

"Who wants you dead? Who's responsible for murdering your party?" Slader rubbed his cold hands together, but still the chill burrowed deep into his bones.

"That's a good question."

"Who benefits most from your death?"

"Kate. She inherits everything."

"Okay. Who benefits if both of you die? And are we talking much money?"

"Millions. Our only close relative is our grandfather, who is in his eighties, so we have both decided to leave the bulk of our estate to the church in Red Creek with the rest to be divided among a few of our favorite charities. So I don't see money as a motive for someone wanting me dead, and believe me, I've been thinking about this."

"Then there's something else you haven't considered. Tell me about your company."

"There's not much to tell. I have three partners, but they don't benefit from my death. Besides, we're good friends. We went to college together and dreamed of having our own business. We started the company ten years ago and have been very successful with a couple of drugs we've developed."

"How about another drug company? I hear the business can be cutthroat."

"The competition to create a new drug is fierce, but I can't see one going so far as to murder me to stop me from contacting the Quentas tribe. The Indians have a few plants they use that might have possibilities, but murder—" Zach shook his head. "I just don't see it. We're a small company."

Slader kept his opinion—that Kate's brother might be too naive—to himself. People killed for a lot of lesser reasons than that every day. When he got back to Mandras, he intended to explore that possibility, because whether Zach wanted it to be or not, this was personal. He wouldn't rest until he got to the bottom of who was trying to kill Kate and him.

Slader looked over at Kate sound asleep in the hammock. Weariness etched her ashen features. If anything happened to her, he wouldn't be able to forgive himself for bringing her into the rain forest. His first instinct had been to get as far away from here as possible, and he should have listened to that inner voice. Now he wasn't sure they would make it back to Mandras alive.

"She knew you were alive. Even when everyone else gave up, she didn't," Slader murmured, wondering what it would feel like to have someone care that much for him. He'd had it once and it had slipped through his fingers because of his ambition, because he'd thought of nothing but the recognition and acclaim he and Renee would receive over the archaeological find.

"Kate and I have a connection," Zach broke into Slader's thoughts. "We've always known when the other is hurting. I guess it's the twin thing."

"When everyone else would have run back to the States and let someone else search for you, she wouldn't. She threw herself into the thick of things even when those men were after us. She said God would protect us."

"Her faith has always been unshakable."

"It sounds like yours has been shaken."

"A few times, but not my Kate. After our parents and sister died…" Zach paused for a few seconds, his voice thick. He cleared his throat and continued, "She turned to the Lord and, as is her way, threw herself into her faith. She's never had one doubt that I know of since the day she rededicated herself to Jesus."

She was so strong, whereas his life had been riddled with doubts, Slader thought as he again peered at Kate. One of her arms flopped over the side of the hammock and dangled down. He made his way to her and carefully placed it back under the netting at her side. Through the mesh, her features looked peaceful as though she could finally rest now that she had found her brother.

Finding her brother had been easy. They still had to get back to Mandras in one piece. That would be the hard job. There was only one way back to the river town and Slick and his men guarded it.

Through the tentacles of sleep, Kate heard giggling and for a few seconds couldn't place where she was. Then the past day came flooding back, and all she wanted to do was surrender to the weariness that still clung to her as the mist had the jungle.

But the sense of being watched penetrated her foggy mind. She had started to open her eyes when a loud shriek pierced the air and something large and furry pounced on her. She screamed, her eyes flying open at the same time she fought the web of netting that held her down with a reddish brown, furry animal on it. Her arms flung outward as the monkey leaped back onto a child's shoulder.

That was when she realized she was circled by a group of Indian children, all staring and laughing at her as she tried to untangle herself from the netting. Keeping a close watch on the reddish brown monkey with a white face, eyes and mouth ringed with black, perched on the child's shoulder, she relaxed her flailing limbs and drew in a calming gulp of air before trying to free herself from the predicament she found herself in.

"Need some help?" Slader said from behind the child with the monkey, amusement in his expression, in his voice.

"Yes, I think I've wrapped myself into a knot."

While he assisted her, she whispered near his ear, "How long have they been there?"

"About an hour."

"An hour!" In her surprise, her voice rose several levels and the children backed away. Immediately Kate regretted scaring them and offered a smile she hoped would reassure the young ones who ranged in ages from, she guessed, three to ten.

"There. That does it," Slader said. "You're a free woman." He took her hand and pulled her up out of the cocooning hammock.

She spied the gash at the back of his head from the fall down the hill and noticed that it wasn't red. In fact it looked good, considering the limited first-aid kit she'd had available to keep infection from setting in. "In a few days you won't even be able to tell you have a head wound."

"Last night, Zach put some salve on it that he had gotten from the medicine man. Your brother said it works wonders on cuts."

"From the look of your head, it does. Where is that salve? I have some cuts I would like to treat."

Slader pointed to her brother's backpack. "Here. He has been collecting various plants and medicines to take back with him."

Kate sat while Slader took the salve and began smoothing some of it over the cuts she had sustained on her own journey down the hill. The children remained watching and she shifted, feeling as though she were onstage, something she avoided if at all possible.

"Why are they still here?" she finally asked as Slader stuck the salve container back among her brother's items.

"Because you are a novelty to them, sis."

Kate looked around and discovered Zach behind her. "Why?"

"Your hair reminds them of the flames of a fire."

Kate touched the unruly mass. She suspected they had never seen someone with so much curly, thick hair.

One of the children said something to Zach. He laughed. "They would like to feel your hair. May they?"

She scanned the beautiful, curious faces of the nine children and nodded. She was the intruder in their home, so letting them touch her hair was the least she could do.

After each one finished running their fingers through her auburn strands, the eldest child, a girl with long, silky black hair that hung to her shoulders and large expressive dark brown eyes, said something to her. Kate looked at Zach for a translation.

"The best I can tell, she's saying she would like for you to come with her. She wants to show you something."

"Can you tell her later, after we talk?"

When Zach finished explaining to the children, they ran off. "They'll come back later."

"I'm amazed at how well you can communicate with them. You've only been with them two months." Slader shifted closer to Kate while Zach sat cross-legged across from them.

"I pick up languages quickly. I have an ear for them. Their language has some similarities to a few I already knew, but it's different from any other in the Amazon that I have encountered. I still have trouble, but each day I'm learning more about them and their culture."

"You are planning to go back with us?" Kate couldn't keep alarm from lacing her question. She wouldn't feel her brother was safe until he was back home.

"Yes, of course. I won't send you back without me to face what's going on. I'll return here when things are settled concerning who's trying to kill us. Slader and I talked last night. He filled me in on what's been going on. I can't imagine who'd want to see me—us—dead."

"The rainy season will start soon and we need to find a way back to Mandras," Slader said with a glance around him. "Do you have any ideas?"

Zach shook his head. "The Quentas can take us to the edge of their territory, but after that we'll be on our own. I think you two need to recuperate a few days, then we'll leave."

"But, Zach, shouldn't we leave tomorrow?" Kate scanned the large hut, taking in everything that was different from what she was used to, feeling so out of place in this world. She wanted her familiar surroundings back. This one adventure would last her a lifetime.

"Kate, I need a little more time. The first four weeks here I was in bad shape from the gunshot wound and the other injuries that I sustained. I'm just getting my own strength back to make the long trek to Mandras. That will give me enough time to complete my gathering of plants."

She knew the truth in her brother's words. She hadn't been up but an hour and already she was tired and wanted to rest again. The jungle had a way of zapping a person's energy and hers had run dry in the days it had taken to get here. Just the thought of going back exhausted her.

"Can I help with your gathering?" Kate asked, not sure what was expected of her and Slader in this new environment. In Red Creek, she knew and couldn't wait to get back to her dull routine.

"No, I'm working with the medicine man which I've discovered is an honor not bestowed on many. He's the one who saved me from near death. I think he feels responsible for me now."

"What can we do?" Kate slid her gaze to Slader. She couldn't get the idea that they were a team out of her mind.

Zach rose. "Explore the area. This is a beautiful part of the jungle. When the little girl comes back, she wants to show you where the women wash. Go with her. It's a pool set aside for the women of the tribe. No men allowed."

Kate remembered the other pool she had washed off in with Slader. That was when their relationship had begun to change, to what she wasn't sure. In her heart she felt he was more than a friend, but what? They were just too different for there to be anything more between them than friendship, and yet she felt so close to him after their time spent on the hill.

Later that day, Kate came back into the hut, re-freshed, clean, almost feeling new again. She started for Zach's hammock, and noticed her brother was nowhere to be found, but Slader paced in front of the mat he had slept on the night before. His expression held an excitement that electrified the air about him.

He caught sight of her and stopped, a broad smile on his face that reached deep into his eyes. "Did you enjoy your bath?"

"Yes. Zach's right. The jungle on this plateau is glorious. I feel as if we're in a story about a lost world."

Slader clasped her hand. "Perhaps we are. I have something to show you."

He framed her face with his hands and planted a deep kiss on her mouth that took her by surprise. When he leaned away, the zeal barely contained in him spread to encompass her. She smiled what she was sure was a silly grin, as though she were a teenager again and being courted by the most popular guy in school.

"What do you want to show me?" she asked as he tugged her outside.

"You'll see."

Behind another long hut there stood a tall round pole with figures and markings faded with time, carved into it. Slader swept his arm toward it. "These markings are from the Inca culture. The symbols are similar to others I've seen at Inca sites in Peru. I've never heard or seen anything like this from other tribes in the Amazon."

"What does it mean?"

"When I saw this pole, I discovered that this tribe moves with them when they change their village location and I began exploring like Zach said." Again, Slader took her hand and strode toward the jungle in the opposite direction from the women's bathing pool.

After walking along a worn path, under the thick canopy for twenty minutes, the trail ended at the base of a huge stone structure that was overgrown with vegetation. Now the trees hemming it in towered over it as though cradling it from the world.

"I think I found my Inca civilization in the Amazon. I think the Quentas are their ancestors. I'll have to do some more exploring and have Zach ask questions for me to confirm that." Grinning from ear to ear, he spread his arms wide, his expression full of life. "But in my gut, I know this is what I had been looking for all those years ago."

Kate snapped her gaping mouth closed. It was incredible. When she thought about how isolated the Quentas were and how different their lifestyle was, it was a definite possibility they could be the remnant of a lost civilization of Incas who had fled the Spanish conquerors.

"God has given you back your life, your purpose," Kate said.

Slader swung around and faced her, the fervor gone from his expression. "No, God has nothing to do with this. This is pure dumb luck."

"I don't believe anything happens by chance. So what are you going to do about this?"

His features again showing his earlier zeal, Slader touched a large stone with moss growing on it. "I don't know. I just found it. But it does complicate things."

"With whom? You with your self-imposed exile?"

He stepped back as if her words had struck him. The joy that had been carved into his features only a moment before vanished, replaced with anger. "What do you want from me?"

"To be honest with yourself. Why is it people always blame God for everything that goes wrong?"

"If, as you say, your God exists, then doesn't He have the power to control everything? And therefore He is the cause when things go wrong?" Slader's voice was lethally quiet, barely heard over the chatter of a troop of monkeys high in the trees.

"God created us to think for ourselves. We aren't puppets merely performing a play to His dictation. What kind of life would that be? Is that what you want, no free will?"

His eyes narrowed, his hands at his side clenching and unclenching.

"I once read a story about a computer that decided everything for people. What kind of job they would hold. Who they would marry and when. Human error was taken out of their life. Do you think that would bring back Renee and your baby? Is that really what you want—to have no choices?"

"Yes." His one-word answer blasted her in the face.

She moved into his personal space, toe to toe with him. "It doesn't work that way. Going through life, you will make mistakes. Hopefully you'll learn from them."

"You've retreated from men because of what happened when you were a teenager and your fight with your sister. Isn't there something in your Bible that talks about casting the first stone?"

His words hurt. Yet, she realized, she was doing the same with him. She had handled this all wrong.

Lord, Slader is right. Please help me to understand the man and help him to see Your forgiveness, even if he can't forgive himself for what happened to his wife and child, even if he can't forgive You for taking them from him.

The instant she finished her prayer, she realized something that Slader had been trying to get her to see. She hadn't forgiven herself about Tess. She was doing exactly what he was doing—hiding from life, not living fully, because she didn't think she deserved to, not after the fight she'd had with her sister.

He released a long breath. "I shouldn't have said that."

She looked him in the eye. "Yes, you should have. It appears as though neither one of us can move on with our lives because of our pasts. When do you think we've done enough penance to forgive ourselves?"

One corner of his mouth quirked. "That's the million dollar question."

"Do you think Tess or Renee would be pleased with how we have lived our lives?"

Slader's forehead furrowed. "Renee would have chewed me out."

"I don't think Tess would be happy with—"

"There you two are." Zach approached them on the path with the Indian girl who had shown Kate the women's bathing pool earlier. "Ah, I see you found the ruin."

"Do you know anything about the Inca civilization?" Slader asked, a silent message in his eyes that said he and Kate would talk later.

"You think this ruin is Incan?"

"A strong possibility. I would need to do some digging around. I'm really not equipped for what I would need to do to authenticate it as belonging to the Incan culture, but I'll do what I can. Is this the only stone structure?"

"Yes, at least visible. But, as you can see, the jungle reclaims the land quickly after a place is abandoned."

Kate listened to her brother and Slader discuss the building and the possibility it was Incan with Slader filling Zach in about his credentials as an archaeologist. She saw the excitement return to Slader's expression. She heard it in his voice.

"There's going to be a feast tonight in honor of the woman with hair of fire and the man with eyes the color of a black jaguar nearby."

"There is one close by?" Kate searched the surrounding rain forest, suddenly feeling confined.

Zach laughed. "You don't need to worry, sis. Jaguars usually sleep during the day. It's rare to see one. They stay hidden."

"Good. I would love to see one, but I'm afraid at a zoo is about all I can take."

"Your sister doesn't do snakes, rats, bugs, spiders or caiman." Slader counted off, using his fingers.

"Oh, that's too bad," Zach said, shaking his head. "We're having rat tonight for dinner. It's roasting right now over the fire."

ELEVEN

"A rat? As in one will feed this whole tribe?" Kate remembered the rat she had seen in the alley as she and Slader had fled Slick the first time. It was big but not *that* big.

His lips pressed together, Zach kneaded the back of his neck. "Actually you don't need but one or two capybaras to feed this tribe unless you're extra hungry. I seem to remember you have a healthy appetite."

Kate playfully hit her brother's arm, which sent the Indian girl into giggles. "That's not a rat."

"It's a rodent. It's a member of the same order of gnawing mammals, Rodentia."

"Count yourself lucky, Slader, that you don't have a genius for a brother," Kate said with a huff and started back toward the village with the girl.

"I wish we could stay a little longer with the Quentas," Kate said as dawn broke two mornings later. Over the short time they had been there, she had learned a lot about the tribe and the jungle they lived so harmoniously with. She hated to think about what lay ahead for them when they left the Quentas and had to face Slick and his cohorts. But time didn't stand still and sooner or later they needed to discover who was trying to kill them.

Zach stuffed the last items into his backpack, then slung it over his shoulder. "We'll slip by Slick and his men. There's much to do when we get back to Mandras."

Taking Zach's machete in his hand, Slader grabbed Kate's pack. "Our guides are ready." He nodded toward the entrance of the long hut. "Are you ready, Kate?"

"Yes."

"Then let's do this." Slader motioned for Zach to go first with Kate next and him last.

The easy pace their two Quentas guides set allowed Kate to keep up. She still perspired quite a bit, but she actually thought her body was getting used to the humidity. And the past few days' rest had helped a lot. By midmorning, when Zach had the Indians stop for a break, she didn't fall to the ground, but managed to ease down onto a log in a somewhat ladylike movement. She swallowed several gulps of water from her canteen then passed it to Slader.

He tipped it back and drank. Kate watched, the whole time thinking her lips had just touched the same place his did and would again. A thrill shot through her, especially when she began remembering the kisses they had shared. What would it be like to share another one? Up until that moment she had been handling the heat just fine. All of a sudden it felt ten degrees hotter and sweat coated her face even more than usual. How was she going to handle not seeing Slader when she returned to Red Creek?

"You okay?" Slader asked, handing her back the canteen.

She took another few sips, trying desperately not to think about his lips, his kisses. "I'm just hunky-dory," she replied, less than successful in her endeavor.

He gave her a strange look, as though he could read her thoughts and knew she wasn't really hunky-dory. "If you say so. The pace is all right?"

She nodded, deciding after using a word like *hunky-dory,* she should keep her mouth shut. Where was her thesaurus when she needed it? At home safe on her bookshelf. *Safe.* She'd forgotten what that word meant. When she returned to Red Creek, would all this seem like a dream, including her feelings for Slader? Somehow she doubted it.

"We need to get moving," Zach said, and rose.

Slader pulled Kate to her feet and stopped her from following her brother with a hand on her arm. She turned to him, arching one brow in question.

"Something's wrong. I can feel it."

"You have that itch again?" Kate searched the area, half-expecting the four men looking for them to come charging out of the jungle.

"No, not that." He shook his head, plowing his hand through his damp hair. "I just sensed something from you. I thought maybe something was wrong. Must be my imagination."

It was *her* imagination that was getting her into

trouble, not his. Kate kept her mouth shut this time and spun around to hurry after Zach and the two Quentas guides. But for the rest of the day, she kept from thinking about what it would be like if Slader kissed her again.

At the end of the day, Kate collapsed at the edge of the river that marked the Quentas territory. She was in better shape than when she'd begun, but not that good that she wasn't affected by the heat and humidity. The two Indians went into the jungle to hunt for some food while Zach and Slader set up the camp and retrieved wood for the fire. Kate had started to rise to help with the preparations when Slader waved her down.

"We can handle it." Slader lit the wood.

"But—"

"I've been in the Amazon a lot longer than you and have learned to deal with the climate. Kate, you have nothing to prove to me. You've been amazing on this trip."

She beamed, feeling the effect of his words from the top of her head to the tip of her toes. She was sure she was glowing so much that she could have been a beacon directing their pursuers to them. "So I can just kick back and be a woman of leisure then?"

"Sounds good to me."

His light tone set the mood for the rest of the evening while they enjoyed a roasted bird. The two Quentas offered to stand watch, so Kate curled up in Zach's hammock while both men slept on the ground not far from her. Exhausted, she went to sleep right away, but images of Slick and his buddies invaded her dream. Some time in the middle of the night, with sweat drenching her, she jackknifed straight up in the hammock with her mosquito netting a veil about her.

The usual jungle noises greeted her and calmed her frantically beating heart. For a few seconds she couldn't get the picture of Slick with his knife blade planted across her neck out of her mind. Slowly, she began to see what was really before her. Slader sat by the fire, having obviously put some more wood on it, because it was going strong. The two Indian guides were alert at the edge of the jungle.

"Kate? What's wrong?"

Slader's question, full of gentle query, wafted to her, causing her to recall another part of her dream, the part where Slader kissed her again. She inhaled deeply and held the breath for a few seconds. "Nothing. Just a bad dream."

"Then go back to sleep."

The jolt of coming awake suddenly wiped any desire to sleep from her mind. She swung her legs to the ground and stood. Making her way to the fire, she sat next to Slader and picked up a stick beside her. The scent of smoke blended with the aroma of moldy vegetation, searing her nostrils with the stench.

"Can't sleep," she said. "You're stuck with me. Why aren't you sleeping?" Kate drew circles in the dirt by her feet, aware of the sounds of rushing water and the constant monotonous drone of insects, with an occasional pierce of an animal's call.

"Can't. Trying to figure out the best way to make it back to Mandras in one piece."

"Come up with a plan yet?"

"We're staying off the river and going by land, which won't be easy."

"You don't have to worry about me. I can do it." She tossed the stick to the ground.

He chuckled. "I knew you would say that. Then I'll worry about myself. I know how hard it will be and going by land doesn't guarantee we won't run into Slick and his pals."

"We haven't come this far not to make it to Mandras."

"Because your God is going to protect us?"

"Yes," Kate said instantly, knowing that in every fiber of her being. "You believed once, so He was your God, too. Has being angry at Him solved your problem, made you feel better?"

His mouth curved down in a frown. "I'm just hunky-dory."

Kate winced at the expression she'd used earlier. "Who are you really angry with, yourself or God?"

"Why aren't you mad? He took your family away from you?"

"Death is a part of this life. Believing in God was what made it bearable for me, because I'll be reunited with them one day. If I hadn't had God to turn to for solace, then I…" She shuddered at the thought of her life without the Lord and His love.

Slader took the stick Kate had dropped and began to make his own circles, staring at the ground by his feet.

"I have the feeling your life isn't what you've

wanted for some time, so obviously getting angry at God hasn't solved anything for you. Maybe you should try talking to Him again."

"You mean praying?"

His question held no anger, only soft inquiry. "Well, yes and no. I pray, but I also have conversations with Him. There are no secrets between us."

"What time is?" Zach asked behind Kate, his voice laced with sleep.

She checked her waterproof watch, a constant reminder of the civilization they were returning to. "It's about an hour before dawn."

"Why are you all up then?"

Kate turned at the same time as Slader and they both replied, "Can't sleep."

Zach stretched, then rose and stretched some more. "I guess I'll join you. What were you two talking about?"

Before Kate could tell her brother, Slader asked, "Have you given any more thought to who might want you dead?"

Zach settled across from Kate and Slader. "I don't know."

"Tell me about your business partners. We have an hour to kill."

"I have three of them, but it can't be one of them. It must be a rival drug company, but even that is hard to believe." Shaking his head, Zach laced his hands together and leaned forward, resting his elbows on his thighs.

Kate knew how hard this was for her brother. They

had grown up in a small town, sheltered from the harsh realities of the world, and even though he now lived in Dallas—a two-hour drive from Red Creek—murder and attempted murder weren't something he was used to.

"We're each in change of a different facet of the company. Anthony Hansom is the president and oversees the global picture. Mark Nelson runs the sales division. Chad Thomas runs the accounting department. I'm research and development. I went to college with all three. Anthony is a deacon at my church in Dallas. Mark and I were childhood friends, and Chad and I were roommates for four years in college. I have known these men well for a long time. So, no, I don't have any idea who would want me dead nor why."

"If we don't discover who before you return to Dallas, you will have a big bull's-eye on your chest."

Kate shivered and unconsciously slid closer to Slader on the log. "What do you suggest we do?"

"Before you two leave Mandras, find out who hired Slick." Slader covered her hand on the log between them.

"Will you help us?" Kate relished the warmth of his touch. Reassuring. Comforting when her own world at the moment was unfamiliar, threatening.

"I thought you'd never ask. Yes, I'll help. This is personal now. They tried to kill me."

Three hours later, Slader returned from his scouting trip. "Just as we left them. Two of them are still guarding the river below the waterfall."

"Where is Slick and his friend?" Kate asked, inspecting the green undergrowth around her as though any second Slick and his pal would emerge.

"Good question. Probably waiting upstream."

"So if we get past these men, we are home free?"

"Maybe."

"Meaning?" Kate's anxiety skyrocketed.

"Slick may be downstream waiting. One thing is for sure. He hasn't given up."

"Why not?" Kate asked. Living on the edge the past few weeks had taken its toll on her. Stress knotted her muscles and caused her stomach to churn.

"He's like an anaconda. He doesn't let go once he has you in his grip, and he thinks he's got us in his grip."

"What do we do?" Zach's grasp on his machete tightened as though he were preparing for battle.

The image of her brother going into battle unnerved Kate. She wanted her old, safe life back, but there was a part of her that realized her old life came without Slader and she desperately wanted to hold on to this time with him. The simple truth was she loved him. After thirty-eight years, she had allowed herself to fall in love with someone who wasn't a possible mate.

"I know these two. They aren't particularly smart. We'll take care of them tonight, which—" Slader glanced toward the sky that was obscured by the canopy of trees above him "—will be upon us soon."

"How?" Kate asked, feeling as though she were trapped like the prey of that anaconda. She needed to stay focused on the conversation, not on the fact she loved a man who still mourned his dead wife.

Tired lines deep in his features, Slader rubbed his

hands down his face. "I don't know yet. Got any suggestions?"

Slader's presence next to her calmed her fragile nerves and gave her the courage to propose her plan to capture the two men. "As a matter of fact, I do."

Slader's eyes grew wide while Zach's quiet laughter spiced the air. "My sister always has an opinion."

"Don't I know it."

For a few seconds, Kate forgot about the men after them, forgot about her brother only a couple of feet away, and riveted her attention on Slader as though he were the only other person alive. The frail bond between her and Slader should have surprised her, but his vulnerability was much like hers. She had seen his interest in why she believed so fervently. Perhaps there had been two reasons for her trip to the Amazon—to save Zach and to save Slader.

Dear Heavenly Father, please protect us from harm and help us to get back to Mandras in one piece. Look out for Zach and Slader and don't let them do anything foolish. And, Lord, allow Slader to see the wisdom in my plan.

Slader's expression of exasperation made her smile as he waited for her to reveal her plan. "Maybe I could lure them—"

"Absolutely not," Slader cut in, his weary expression evolving into an angry one. "I'm not letting you put yourself in danger."

Kate stood directly in front of Slader, waving one arm around to indicate the jungle that hemmed them in on all four sides. "You don't think I am in danger right this moment? The second I took up this adventure, I was in danger and until we can solve the mystery of who is trying to kill us and put that person behind bars, I will continue to be in danger. So," she inhaled a deep breath, "I can go into their camp as though I am lost and no one is left of the expedition. For that matter, we don't even know if these two men know what I look like. They may think I'm someone else. This could throw them off enough to let you two overtake them."

Slader's eyes became pinpoints as he glared down at her, his arms stiff at his sides. "It has possibilities, but I would like to change things up a bit. Here's what I think."

Thirty minutes later after all the kinks were worked out of the plan, Slader motioned Kate and Zach through the jungle toward the two pursuers' campsite. On the outskirts of their camp Slader positioned himself to watch and wait with Kate on one side of him and Zach on the other.

Dark blanketed the jungle except for the blaze of the fire the two men kept feeding with wood. They glanced around every few minutes and stayed near the blaze as though they knew they were being watched and it offered some protection. The bigger of the two men had his automatic rifle slung over his shoulder while the other's lay propped up against the log he sat on.

Slader prayed, *God, it's been five long years since I've asked You for anything, but please protect Kate. This crazy plan just might work, but if she's right, we need You on our side. She believes in You and trusts that*

You will get us through this alive. I—the world can't lose her.

Slader's first prayer in years muttered silently in his mind had come surprisingly easy for him. And even stranger was the fact it felt right to him.

The bigger man rose and stretched, saying in Spanish to the other one that he needed to take care of business. Now that it was dark and unlikely that people would be traveling on the river, Slader was sure both men felt there wasn't anything to threaten them but the dangerous animals of the night.

"This is our cue. Ready," Slader muttered, looking at Kate.

Her shirt buttoned all the way to the top, she took a moment to undo two of the buttons and then to bend over, fluffing her hair before tossing it back behind her. "How do I look? Helpless?"

Although Slader saw her strength and self-confidence, for a second doubts plagued him. The plan wouldn't work. Kate wouldn't look lost and alone, helpless. Then she ripped one of her sleeves so it hung off her shoulder and smeared more dirt into her clothes and on her face. He nodded, gesturing her to go before he lost his nerve with their plan and pulled her back into the safety of his arms.

Wetting her lips, Kate slunk into a standing position in the middle of the undergrowth. She took several short puffs of air, then charged forward. She hoped Slader wasn't feeding her a line about her hair being beautiful down in a curly array of red brown. She had never used the fact she was a woman to lure a man to do anything.

She wasn't sure she knew how, but she was determined to do her part in getting them back to Mandras. The Lord and her resolve gave her courage to keep moving forward.

"Socorro! Todos están muertos," she gasped, using the Spanish phrase Zach had taught her after they had finalized the plans. Even though they were still technically in Brazil, they weren't far from the border, and it was apparent from their earlier conversation these two spoke Spanish.

The tall, reed-thin man shot to his feet, his dark eyes as round as the full moon of the night before. He stared at her, not making a move toward his gun as she stumbled toward him.

"Socorro!" She fell at his feet, near the gun. She wasn't sure she could pick up the weapon, having always abhorred guns of any kind, but she could keep him from getting his hands on it if her body was in the way.

A scuffing sound coming from the jungle alerted the slender man that something wasn't right. He turned to peer behind him and reached for the automatic rifle at the same time. Kate bit down hard on the inside of her cheek and flew upward, her fists connecting with his soft stomach before he had a chance to complete his move. Air whooshed out of him as his eyes widened.

Slader led the bigger man into the camp at gunpoint, his hands laced together behind his head. Slader shouted something at the slim guy Kate dubbed *Laurel* after Laurel and Hardy fame, then she motioned him to step away from Kate and the other gun. With his arms crossed over his midsection, the slender one sidled a few feet toward the fire.

"Get the gun, Kate."

"Do I have to?" Just the thought of touching something so deadly gave her the creeps.

"Yes." Slader practically growled the one word at her.

Kate saw herself as though she were moving in slow motion as she reached for the automatic rifle. Gripping the hard barrel, she heaved it up into her arms and cradled it like a baby.

"Now bring it over here." Slader never removed his gaze from either of the two men whom he had herded together on one side of the fire.

Kate, too, kept her attention trained on both Laurel and Hardy. The more she looked at them, the more she thought her names for them were appropriate. Hardy was big and massive with a round belly that his dirt-stained T-shirt didn't completely cover, whereas Laurel's limbs reminded her of bamboo poles sticking out of his shirt and shorts. Besides, she found it much easier to think of them as the famous comic team rather than two men trying to hunt them down to kill them.

Slader relieved her of her rifle, shouldering it behind him, all the while watching Laurel and Hardy. "See if you can find something to tie them up with."

Kate noticed their packs on the ground near their hammocks. In one hammock, covered up by the mosquito netting was a satellite phone sticking out partway. She ignored it and dragged the backpacks nearer the fire. She wrinkled her nose at the moldy smell that assaulted her as she rummaged through the first one. Judging by the size of the shirt she pulled out, she guessed it was Hardy's belongings, and he definitely needed lessons in how to take care of his clothes. Mold on his shirt gagged her throat, threatening to cut off the air to her lungs. She dropped the offending piece of clothing and hesitantly delved deeper into the bag.

"Dump the contents on the ground."

Slader's simple suggestion had been so obvious, but old habits were hard to break. She had never gone through another person's possessions, and she couldn't shake the funny feeling she was intruding on his privacy.

Turning the backpack over, she shook the contents free. Disappointment hunched her shoulders when she saw nothing that could be used to tie up their captives. She moved to Laurel's bag. Dumping his belongings on the ground, she spied some rope and let out a squeal of delight. You would think she had found a Gutenberg Bible by her giddy response. She held up the rope.

"I want you to hold this gun on them while I tie them up."

Slader's request sent panic through her. Hold the gun? On the men? "I don't think that would be a good idea."

"After what I've seen you do these past few weeks, you can do this, Kate."

The confidence in his deep, husky voice eased her misgivings until he placed the cold, hard metal in her hands. Then she nearly dropped the gun because her palms were so sweaty. Gripping the rifle tighter, she aimed it toward Laurel and Hardy. She prayed they didn't see her shaking and rush Slader and her.

With the other rifle strapped across his back, Slader approached Laurel first, cut the rope in half with his machete and quickly had the slim man tied up like a wild boar. He lay on the ground with his hands and feet bound together behind his back. Next came Hardy, who threw punches at him until Slader struck him in the jaw. Hardy's dazed state gave Slader the opening he needed. Shoving the large man down onto the ground, Slader went about tethering his hands and ankles together, too.

The whole time Kate held the gun, which shook visibly now. Once Hardy was bound, she quickly relinquished her tight grasp on it and lowered it to her side.

Slader grabbed it before her loose hold caused it to fall to the ground. "Ready," he whispered for her ears only.

She gave him a slight nod.

He spun about and pointed the gun at the large man, telling him in English, "You know, the more I think about it, the more I think we should kill them. Why keep them alive? It's a long night and I don't want to have to worry about them." His fierce tone and emphasis on the words *kill* and *alive* made the two men blink as fear invaded their expressions.

Laurel and Hardy might not know English, but they understood the substance of what they were talking about. Sweat glistened on their faces and soaked their shirts.

"You can't kill them!" Kate gestured wildly at them. "Please, Slader."

Slader took a menacing step toward Laurel. "Why not? They are scum. They wanted us dead."

Again the word *dead* had a visible effect on both bound men. Hardy tried to scoot away, while Laurel bucked and twisted against his restraints.

Slader waved the gun and shouted, "Stop."

Hardy froze. Laurel grew still.

"See what I mean? Trouble. Not worth our time." Slader turned away from Laurel and Hardy to give Kate a quick wink they couldn't see.

She almost laughed and spoiled the little drama they had planned for the two men. She pressed her lips together to keep the smile that threatened inside.

When Slader raised the rifle to aim at the large one on the ground again, Kate stepped in front of him and blocked his shot. "No! You can't. I won't let you."

Slader glared at her for a long moment, then blew out a rush of air and lowered his weapon. He stalked to the log and sat with the rifle cradled in his lap. As planned, Kate went to comfort him while he continued to watch the two captives. Laurel shook as badly as she had when she held the weapon. Behind Hardy's glare, fear lurked. Sweat coated his stained shirt and flowed in rivers off his face. Kate hoped neither man would try to escape, which might force Slader to shoot them.

As she sat next to Slader she could tell by the strained lines on his face that their little drama had cost him. She remembered he had been in the Gulf War and she wondered about his time as a soldier. Had this scene brought back memories he had wished to forget?

"Are you all right?" she asked in a low voice that the crackling of the fire and the jungle sounds masked.

"Having this automatic rifle in my hand reminds me that I know how to use it. Have been trained to use it well."

"I figured that."

He shot her a look of surprise.

"I think you and I have gotten to know each other well these past few weeks."

His gaze swung back to the two captives. "I guess you're right."

"Does that bother you?"

"I should say yes, but strangely it doesn't."

"I would have thought, by the kind of life you've been leading, you would be used to violence."

"Not if I can help it. When I go into the jungle I carry a shotgun for protection and to hunt for food. And the protection isn't usually from man, but from animals." He sent a scowl toward the men. "When I was drinking heavily after Renee's death, I got quite a bad reputation. I suppose that has kept the riffraff from bothering me, which in this case works to our advantage. After that little display, I doubt they will test me."

This time Kate averted her face and smiled at Slader's feigned fierceness. "We have a few hours to kill."

"Don't say that word too loudly. They'll think you've changed your mind."

Resting her elbows on her thighs, Kate ducked her

head and massaged her neck. "You didn't tie them up too tight that they can't get loose, did you?"

"Why, Kate, you doubt my abilities?"

"No, but they look like they aren't going anywhere."

"They aren't for a while. After we take their canoe tomorrow, though, I bet they are untied in an hour or so."

"I hope so. I don't want to wait forever for Slick to show up. We have a murderer to catch. Hopefully the guy in Mandras who hired Slick will have a name for us."

"Maybe."

"You don't think he will?"

"Too easy, but maybe we'll get lucky."

Father, please let this end soon. Red Creek seems a world away and I guess it is. I need to get back to my life where I'm not fighting off wild animals and fleeing bad guys.

"How long have they been free?" Kate asked Zach the next morning when she crouched down next to her brother, who had stayed back to keep an eye on Laurel and Hardy at their campsite where they had been tied up.

"Fifty minutes and they immediately put in a call to Slick, who is on his way back."

"Good. Now all we have to do is wait." Slader settled in next to Kate.

"Where did you stash the canoe?" Zach asked.

"About a hundred yards down the river. I didn't want to lose too much time having to track through the jungle when we leave."

Kate, buffered with Slader on one side and Zach on the other, felt about as safe as she could in their situation. Slader handed the other rifle to Zach, who surprisingly took it and acted as if he knew what he was doing with it. When had her brother learned to use one?

She turned her attention to Laurel and Hardy. Hardy paced around the fire pit while Laurel kept his attention glued to the river. She doubted Slick would be very happy with them.

"Lord, please protect these two men from Slick's wrath," she murmured.

"Praying for the enemy?" Slader whispered into her ear.

His breath washed over her neck, its warmth fanning outward and sending a shiver that rippled through her body. "Yes, it's the right thing to do."

He gave her a puzzled look and resumed his watch on the campsite.

Her legs aching from squatting, she shifted, intending to kneel instead. As she glanced down, fear shook her very foundation. She opened her mouth to scream.

TWELVE

Slader immediately clamped a hand about Kate's mouth before her scream shrilled the air. Her heart thumped against her rib cage in triple time as she watched the *huge* scorpion crawl over her boot and disappear into the underbrush in front of her. Rivulets of sweat rolled down her face, collecting where Slader's hand still clasped her.

Slowly, as though he wasn't sure if she would scream, he released her, gripping her shoulder in silent support as she collapsed back against him. All she could think about was the scorpion, over four inches long, on her boot and that it had a deadly sting. Of course, she hadn't considered the fact that she wore thick leather boots that protected her feet. But still, the poisonous creature had been on her!

Slader put his lips against her earlobe and whispered, "It's gone. Okay?"

With the feel of his breath on her neck, she nodded.

He brought his arms around her and hugged her. Still clasped in his embrace, she continued to observe the scene in the campsite, wishing she could stay there indefinitely. But a few minutes later Slader released her and resumed his vigil.

What would happen after they found the person behind the attempts on their lives? Kate wondered. Would Slader go back to the site of the Inca ruins to fulfill a lifelong dream? Would he forget her? The very thought saddened her, and yet how could they ever be together? His lack of faith would always be a barrier.

Several hours later, Slick and his toady pulled their canoe up onto the beach by the encampment. Seeing Slick, Kate tensed and Slader again clamped her shoulder in support, his hand massaging her. For a few seconds, she surrendered to his soothing touch as she came to grips with the sight of the blond giant, armed to the teeth with a machete and a large knife at his waist and an automatic rifle in his hands.

Slick starting yelling and even struck Hardy with the butt of his rifle. Laurel stood off to the side, not daring to get close, and mumbled some words. Then Slick turned his attention to the slender man and walked toward him. Laurel held up his hands and pleaded. Kate didn't have to understand the language to follow what was going on between the men.

Finally Slick motioned with the gun for Laurel and Hardy to get into the canoe. Slick sat in the middle with his rifle ready at a second's notice. Then the toady pushed it off from the bank and hopped into it, taking a paddle along. The current took them out of sight quickly.

Kate sagged back, every muscle having been locked

into place through the whole scene with Slick. Now all she wanted to do was sleep from the exhaustion that had become so much a part of her life of late.

"What did they say?" Kate asked while Zach rose from their hiding place.

Slader followed suit, helping Kate to her feet. "Slick doesn't think we found your brother. He thinks we're back in Mandras and he intends to find us."

A shudder trembled down her length. "You were right to suggest Zach stay out of sight."

"I'm counting on Slick heading straight for the Blue Dolphin. I think that's where we'll find him and I'm hoping he'll be alone. Let's get moving. He won't wait forever. We need to be in place outside the bar when he decides I'm not showing up. I'm hoping he'll lead us to the man who hired him."

"I thought I told you to stay at the hotel," Slader muttered in such a fierce tone Kate stepped back.

"You did. I chose not to listen to you."

"What's new. You're the most exasperating female."

"You're just figuring that out," Zach said with humor in his voice.

Kate placed a hand on her hips and met Slader's frown with one of her own. "I am *not* staying back at the hotel by myself, not when there are people still after us."

"Shh." Slader waved her quiet and peered around the side of the wooden building toward the Blue Dolphin. "He's leaving the bar. Come on with us, but stay back out of danger. I haven't gone through all we've gone through in the past two weeks since you hired me to have something happen to you now."

His voice, pitched low, sent a wave of chills rippling down her, but she wouldn't return to the hotel, and if she could help Slader and her brother, she would. This was her fight, too. Her life had been placed in jeopardy, too.

Up ahead, Slick paused, looked around, then ducked into a seedy one-story structure near the pier. Now it looked deserted with a boarded-up window and missing pieces of the tin roof.

With his hands balled, Zach asked, "How long do we give Slick before we go in and find out who is behind this?"

"Not a second longer. Let's crash this little party." Slader strode toward the building, anger in every line of his body.

Kate trailed the two men, making sure she kept back for the time being, but she had her own questions for whoever was behind hiring Slick. Outside the door, Slader halted, withdrawing a revolver from his waistband. Her gaze fastened onto the gun. Suddenly her pulse kicked up a notch, and she broke out in a cold sweat.

With an arm out, he barred Kate from going any farther. He placed his forefinger to his lips and shook his head, pushing her toward the side of the dilapidated structure. He motioned to the ground at her feet.

She clamped her lips together and watched as Slader and her brother entered the building. Part of her wanted to be inside with them, but she knew she would be a liability in a situation like this. Leaning against the wooden slats, she kept guard on the street in front.

Not five minutes after Slader and Zach had gone inside, Laurel hurried toward the building. Kate straightened, trying to tamp down her fear and panic. She couldn't. It swamped her as though a tidal wave of those emotions had washed over her.

She checked the area for Hardy. Thankfully, Laurel's cohort wasn't around. But that still left the thin man to deal with. He approached the deserted store, quickly opened the door and slipped inside.

What to do? Call the police? Police? The only law in Mandras was the military, manning a post along the river outside of town. Too far for her to get any timely help. That meant she had to do something herself and fast.

Glancing around for a weapon of some kind, she found nothing of use. Trash and broken glass wouldn't be effective against a gun. She hadn't seen one on Laurel, but that didn't mean he didn't have one. She had learned not to assume anything.

She rushed from the side of the building, her heart matching her quick pace as she neared the door. With a trembling hand she turned the knob and eased the door open. She stuck her head inside and peered around. At one time the place had been a store of some kind, but now the shelves and counter were empty and all that greeted her inspection of the front room was dust, insects and cobwebs. She stepped into the building, quietly shutting the door. A musty, moldy smell, like day-old, damp gym socks, accosted her.

She automatically brought her hand to her nose and mouth, wishing she didn't have to breathe.

She heard voices from somewhere in the building but couldn't understand what was being said. There was only one door off the front area so she headed across the wooden planks toward it.

Out of the corner of her eye something green caught her attention. She glimpsed a lizard, its black eyes fixed on her. Jumping away, she nearly screamed. This time she swallowed it before any sound escaped. The iguana darted behind the counter. Now her heart thudded so loudly she was sure the men in the back could hear her approach. Before moving again, she checked around for any other creatures that might surprise her.

Someone speaking Portuguese raised his voice, prodding Kate forward. At the door she inched it open and found Laurel in a hallway listening. Kate retreated and scanned the front room for a weapon of any kind. All she saw was a piece of wood, six inches wide and two feet long, on the counter where the iguana had disappeared.

*God, lizards are reptiles like snakes. Please don't make me go over there and get that board. I—*Kate halted her prayer. The sight of the wood reminded her of that time in the alley with Slick. It had worked once. Maybe it would again. In that moment she realized the Lord was making her face some of her worst fears in this journey to the Amazon. Going to where the iguana was hiding was just another fear she needed to overcome. He was with her. She had made it this far with His help. She would accomplish what she needed to do with the Lord by her side.

With that thought, Kate marched over and snatched up the board. A flash of green sank behind the counter and vanished from sight. She hurried back, armed and ready to make sure Laurel didn't mess up the meeting.

Carefully, to make sure she didn't give herself away, she peered down the hallway and saw Laurel stick his hand into his pocket. A gun! Kate didn't wait another second but rushed the man, swinging the board toward his head. The sound of wood smacking flesh echoed in the short corridor. She winced as Laurel slumped to the floor. The thumping noise of his body hitting the tile competed with her now-thundering heartbeat.

She dropped the board, giving up the pretense of being quiet, and hurried to the unconscious man. "Please don't be dead," she muttered, reaching out to feel for a pulse.

She heard the door to the room where Laurel had been listening swing open. Her fingertips found his pulse, which was faint but beating. Sighing, she looked up to see Slader standing in the doorway with a murderous expression on his face that quickly evolved into an exasperated one.

"I knew you were trouble the moment you walked into the Blue Dolphin that first day. What part of 'stay outside' did you not understand?"

She could have pointed out to him that he hadn't said those words to her or that she had just saved him from Laurel breaking up their little meeting. No, she kept her mouth shut and rose. "Have you found out who's trying to kill us?"

"No."

"You haven't?" Kate peered around Slader into the room.

Zach held Slick and another man of short stature with long black hair at gunpoint. Neither one looked happy if their scowls and tensed bodies were any indication. But then her brother didn't look pleased, either.

"But we do have a lead," Slader said, stepping over to Laurel on the floor and checking him for weapons.

"He's got a gun in his pocket." Kate moved to the door.

Slader patted Laurel down, then delved into his two front pockets and came up with a dirty rag. "Is this the gun you're talking about?" He held up the piece of cloth.

The heat of a blush suffused her face. "I thought he was reaching for a gun, so I hit him."

"This from a woman who hates guns. Mighty effective." Slader swept his arm down the length of the prone man.

Ignoring the laughter in his eyes, Kate said, "You said we have a lead. What is it?"

"Mr. Kim is from Belém," Slader said, jerking his thumb in the direction of the short man next to Slick. "The money used to pay him was transferred from a bank in Dallas, one of the banks your brother's company uses. Personally, I don't like coincidences, so I'm thinking the trail leads to Zach's company."

No wonder Zach didn't look too pleased. That meant whoever had tried to have them killed was probably involved with his pharmaceutical company. "So what now?"

"We go to Dallas."

"We?" Hope flared inside Kate.

"Yes, Zach, you and me. I told you I was in this till the end. Someone tried to kill us. I don't take kindly to that."

"So you're going with us—back to the States?" She still couldn't believe he would end his self-imposed exile.

"Yes."

Slader, Kate and Zach left the bank in Dallas, having discovered what they needed. Slader opened the car door for Kate, then slid into the seat in front next to Zach. Tension vibrated in the luxurious confines of her brother's Lexus. She placed her purse on the soft tan leather beside her, conscious of the scowl that occupied Zach's face.

"So you think it's Chad?" Kate finally asked when she couldn't take the strained silence another second.

"He's the one in charge of the money and his name was on the paperwork for the Prentice account, so yes I think it's Chad." Zach's hands on the wheel were tight and white knuckled.

"Did you know anything about the Prentice account?"

Her brother's forehead crunched as though deep in thought. "The name sounds familiar, but I don't remember where I've heard or seen it. But you can bet I'll ask Chad about it today."

Kate stiffened. "You're going to confront him, tell him that you think he hired people to kill you? Contact the police. Let them do their job and figure it all out."

"Chad and I were roommates for four years in college. I intend to face him myself. I won't do anything stupid, but this is something I'm going to handle personally."

"Slader, talk some sense into my brother. He could get killed. What if Chad has a gun?"

Zach snorted. "I doubt it. He's good at numbers and hiding behind others."

The scorn in her brother's voice chilled her. She almost felt sorry for Chad until she remembered what they had gone through the past weeks. "You can't go alone."

"He isn't. I'm going, too."

Zach threw Slader a look. "You don't have to protect me. I'll be fine. I'm confronting him in the office. What could go wrong?"

"Nothing but I'm coming, too." Slader's steely tone emphasized the uselessness in arguing with him.

Kate remembered Chad Thomas. He had come home with Zach during some of the vacations while her brother had been in college. She had once had a crush on Chad. How could the man she had come to know then, be responsible? Like Zach, she didn't understand, but she didn't have the heart to be in the meeting. The intense turmoil of the past few weeks had finally caught up with her. After their visit to Texhoma Pharmaceutical's main offices, she intended to sleep for days. Her mind already felt as if it were in a fog like the mist that blanketed the jungle some mornings.

When Zach drove into the underground parking garage of Texhoma Pharmaceutical Company, he pulled into the space labeled "Zach Collier" and switched off the engine. On the ride up to the top floor where Chad's office was, both her brother and Slader were silent, lost in their thoughts as though preparing for battle. Crossing her arms, Kate hugged herself, suddenly chilled to the bone.

Soon this would be all over and then what? Go back to her old life? How could she after all that had happened? Nothing would ever be the same, especially with a wounded heart.

The elevator doors swished open. The top floor, where the executives of Texhoma Pharmaceutical had offices, stretched before Kate. Intending to visit with Mrs. Rose, Chad's secretary, Kate walked with her brother and Slader to Chad Thomas's office.

Zach nodded to a few people who wore surprised expressions but didn't stop to chat or break his long, purposeful strides. Even they could see her brother was a man on a mission. As Slader had said, this was personal.

"Mrs. Rose, is Chad in his office?" Zach said.

After the older woman's initial shock wore off, she managed to say, "Yes. Do you want me to tell him you are here, Dr. Collier?" She reached for the phone.

"No." Zach put his hand on hers. "I want to surprise him. Please hold all his calls."

Mrs. Rose's eyes grew round at Zach's hard voice, but she nodded.

Zach thrust open Chad's door and entered his partner's office with Slader. Fury carved deep lines into her brother's face, but what made Kate pause more than anything was the cold look in Slader's eyes. Answers would be had today, one way or another.

As the door closed, in need of some caffeine, Kate decided to get some coffee from the break room down the hall. From the look on Mrs. Rose's face, if she stayed there would be questions. She didn't want to answer any questions that the older woman had and she knew that Slader and Zach could take care of themselves. Kate just wanted everything to be over.

Slader positioned himself near the door, keeping an eye on the man behind the desk.

"Zach!" Chad dropped the pen he held onto his desk. It bounced once, then rolled off onto the carpeted floor. "You're alive!" He leaped to his feet.

"Yes, I am, no thanks to you."

Chad blinked, a blank expression replacing his surprise. "What are you talking about? We spent weeks and thousands of dollars searching for you. We thought when there wasn't any trace of you and your team, that you all were dead."

"You're correct about one thing. The team is dead. I'm not." Zach swept his arm down his body. "As you can see, I'm very much alive and wanting some answers."

"What are you talking about?"

Slader had to give Thomas credit. Either he was a great actor or he genuinely didn't know what Zach was talking about. Slader folded his arms over his chest and lounged back against the door.

"Sit!" Zach commanded in a lethally quiet voice.

"What's going on, Zach? Who's that man?" Chad gestured toward Slader.

"Slader found me when no one you sent could. He and Kate, but you wouldn't know that because Mr. Kim and his henchmen are locked up in a Brazilian jail. We didn't give them the chance to warn you."

"Did the jungle get to you? I don't know what you're talking about. How many times do I have to say it?"

"Of course, you wouldn't admit to knowing a Mr. Kim. That would be admitting you hired him to have me killed."

Chad's face went pale, his mouth hanging open. "Why would I want you dead? We're partners, friends. At least we were."

Doubt flitted across Zach's features. Slader was beginning to wonder if he was the right partner. The back of his neck itched. That was never a good sign.

Zach leaned across the desk, planting his fisted hands on the tan blotter. "Mr. Kim hired some men to follow me into the jungle and make sure I didn't return from my expedition. If it hadn't been for the Quentas intervening, I wouldn't have. Then he tried to stop Kate and Slader from finding me. So you see, someone very badly wanted me dead. And I don't take kindly to that."

Chad worked his mouth for a few seconds, but no words came out. Shaking his head, he ran his hand through his hair. Finally he said, "I'm not the one you should be after. Why would you think I was?" Hurt laced the man's question.

"Because the money trail led back to Texhoma Pharmaceutical. There's an account at our bank that the money came out of and you're the one who set it up. The Prentice account."

"I've never heard of it."

"It's your signature on the paperwork."

"Then it's a forgery."

Kate stepped into the empty break room. Relieved to be alone, she headed for the coffeepot and poured herself some brew. She probably shouldn't stay too long. How long did it take to confront a good friend with his treachery?

Out of Zach's three partners, she had hoped it wasn't Chad and Mark who were involved in trying to kill them. She knew those two whereas Anthony Hansom was only an acquaintance.

What she didn't understand, and she was sure Zach didn't, either, was why? What would have driven Chad to do this? She sank onto a chair at the long table, weariness weakening her legs.

A movement at the entrance caught her attention. Mark Nelson came into the room, halted a few feet in and nearly dropped the files he carried. With eyes wide, he hugged the folders against his chest, never taking his gaze from her.

"Why are you here?" he finally asked in a gruff voice. He cleared his throat and continued, "Did you find Zach?"

She had started to stand to give Mark a hug in greeting, but his question took her by surprise. "Find Zach?" She hadn't told very many people her plans to go to the Amazon to look for her brother. She certainly hadn't told anyone at Texhoma.

Mark's expression became unreadable. "Mom said something to me about you going to Brazil. I just assumed that's what you were doing down there."

His mother helped out at her church so obviously she had discovered her plans, probably through the reverend. "Yes, I found Zach," she said slowly, a sudden thought taking hold. No one at Texhoma had known about her trip to the Amazon except Mark, it would seem, so how had Slick known to stop her?

"He's here?" Mark took a step back, his hands continuing to clutch his folders in a fierce grip.

"He's with Chad right now."

Mark stepped back again. "Why?"

"What's wrong, Mark?"

"Nothing. I just remembered a meeting I need to get to." He started to turn into the hallway.

Kate flew across the room and placed a hand on his arm, getting the itch that Slader always talked about. She had known Mark all her life and something was definitely wrong. "Would that meeting be with Mr. Kim?"

For just a second, fear took hold of Mark's expression until an unreadable mask fell over his features. "Who?"

"What have you done?"

"Nothing." He shook off her grip and hurried toward his office.

Kate rushed toward Chad's. The very thought that Mark, Zach's childhood friend, was behind the murders caused bile to rise into her throat. Why? And yet, it made sense. Mark knew of her trip to look for Zach, not Chad or Anthony. Any of the partners of the company could have opened that account used to pay the henchmen. It wouldn't be hard to fake the papers needed since they had come from the company. The more she thought about it she realized the person responsible wouldn't have used his name to open the Prentice account, just in case something had gone wrong with his plan to kill Kate and Zach. So that left one question. Why did Mark do it?

Kate ignored Mrs. Rose at her desk and shoved open the door into Chad's office. "He didn't do it."

All three men positioned around Chad's desk and looking at Chad's computer screen turned toward Kate.

Slader strode to her. "We figured that out. The money for the Prentice account came from another one. Zach remembers seeing something about it before he left for the Amazon."

"It's Mark. He's in his office." Kate clasped Slader's hand and tugged him toward the door. "We can't let him leave."

Chad picked up the phone. "I'll see if I can stop him. You shouldn't confront him. Leave this to the police."

Chad's voice conveyed the anger he felt at being set up by a so-called partner and friend. After he spoke to security, he announced to them, "Mark's already left."

"How? I mean—I—" Stunned, Kate couldn't put her jumbled thoughts into a coherent sentence.

"I think it's time to inform the police and let them

get to the bottom of this," Slader said, slipping his arm about her shoulders.

Kate sagged against him. "I won't feel safe until he's in custody."

"Why don't you take her back to my place, Slader, while Chad and I take care of letting the police know about this."

"I think that's a good idea," Slader said as he headed toward the door with Kate at his side.

Out in the hallway by the elevator, she faced him. "I'm surprised it's Mark, and yet I'm not when I stop and really think about it. Mark was always jealous of Zach all the way through school in Red Creek. They were best friends, but there were times I felt Mark wasn't always telling the truth. I guess, though, it's always easy to say that looking back."

"You know what they say, hindsight is twenty-twenty."

"Yeah, but what could make Mark throw his life away like he has?"

Slader reached around and punched the Down button. "We'll have to wait and see what the police discover. But is money usually involved."

Kate heard murmurs coming from the living room in Zach's apartment. She tossed back the covers on the guest bed and slipped her feet to the thick carpeted floor. Her brother was home finally, after giving his statement to the police. Flipping on the nightstand lamp, she rose and padded toward the door. She had slept for hours and wished she could rest even longer, but she needed answers.

Before entering the living room, Kate shook her head to clear the haze that shrouded her exhausted mind.

When she entered, her brother and Slader ceased talking. Zach had always tried to protect her, but she had thought with Slader they had gotten past that. She had discovered in the jungle she could take care of herself in even the most alien of environments. The feeling empowered her.

"Don't stop talking on my account," Kate said. "Are the police charging Mark?"

"Yes," Zach answered, his own fatigue in every line of his face.

Kate eased down next to Slader, wanting to seek the warmth of his embrace to help chase away the chill that burrowed deep into her bones every time she thought of Mark's betrayal of Zach and of her. "Why did he do it?"

"Simply put—greed. He has an expensive lifestyle that he wanted to maintain at all costs. He turned to illegal means to get that." Zach surged to his feet and began to pace. "He's deep into a drug cartel that wouldn't let him walk away even if he had wanted. It looks like his activities may take the company down with him."

"Oh, no, Zach." Kate went to her brother, laying her hand on his arm. His company had been so important to him—a way for him to help others with his knowledge. "Why did he go after you?"

"Because I saw some papers I wasn't supposed to see right before I left for the Amazon. The funny thing about it is that I didn't realize what I had seen. If he had left well enough alone, he might not have been discovered for a long while. I've been so busy lately I might not put two and two together. But he panicked and got sloppy." Zach's anger mingled with an underlying sadness at being betrayed by a friend, at all the people harmed by Mark's greed. "If it will make you feel any better, Kate, I don't think Mark wanted you killed. He just wanted you not to look for me. He didn't want any more questions asked about what happened to me and my expedition."

Kate hugged her brother, wishing she could take his pain away. "Is there anything I can do to help?"

"No. You've done more than most. You came after me when everyone else believed I was dead." Zach kissed the top of her head. "Now if you two will excuse me, I'm going to bed. If I get to sleep, I probably won't wake up for a week."

Kate watched her brother trudge from the room. He would need her support over the next several months. *Lord, please help Zach to heal from this betrayal. You have a reason for all that's happened. Help him to see what it is.*

Slader stood. "I'd better go."

"You're leaving?"

"I checked into a hotel not far from here."

Kate hadn't realized she was holding her breath until she released it on a long sigh. "I can drive you in Zach's car if you want."

"I need to walk."

"Then I'll see you tomorrow?" Again her breath

caught in her throat while Slader hesitated in answering.

"I can stop by on my way to the airport," he finally replied.

THIRTEEN

"You're going back to the Amazon so soon? Why?"
Kate bit down on her bottom lip the second the
question came out of her mouth, immediately wishing
she could take it back. She didn't want to appear needy,
but she wasn't ready to say goodbye to Slader.

Would she ever be ready? No. That realization made
her come up short. In the jungle, she had grown to love
Slader, but she had thought when she returned to civilization those emotions would diminish, so she'd
refused to explore them too much. They had been
thrown together in an unreal world fighting for their
lives. Of course, she would develop strong feelings
about the man who had saved her on a number of occasions. She'd had it all figured out in the Amazon.

Now, she wasn't so sure. Now, she had to face living
without Slader and it didn't seem so easy. It didn't
even seem possible.

Moving away from the couch, away from Kate,
Slader stared out the large floor-to-ceiling window that

afforded him a gorgeous view of downtown Dallas with lights that went on for miles and miles in all directions. He was in the middle of a large city, so different from the way he had been living for the past five years.

And he didn't know how to answer Kate's question. When he had stepped off the plane and onto American soil again, he had half expected to experience the overwhelming grief and guilt that had become so much a part of his life for the first few years after his wife and unborn child had died. But he hadn't.

Instead he felt as if God had placed a hand on his shoulder and welcomed him back to the land of the living. He didn't know how to take it. He'd lived with his guilt for so long, he was almost afraid to let it totally go. Then what would he do with himself? Live again?

"Slader?" Kate approached him from behind, her voice a shade unsure, a shade sad. "You've only been here a day. Why are you leaving so soon, Slader?"

She wasn't going to let him leave without an answer. She had never made anything easy for him. From the first she'd demanded so much of him in the jungle. She had demanded he live again and stop wallowing in self-loathing.

"I don't know if I can do this," he finally said, gesturing around him as though to encompass all of Dallas.

"Then come with me to Red Creek. It moves at a much slower pace."

"And do what? I don't belong in a small town."

"What is Mandras? A big city?"

He chuckled. How was he going to pick up his life and go on as if he had never met her? But the thought of being with her panicked him. And the thought of being without her panicked him. He was afraid to fall in love with Kate, to open himself up to that kind of pain again. Fear rose within and pushed him forward.

"I have a lot to do over the next several months. Because of you, I found what I had been looking for in the jungle, the Incan ruins."

"So you're going back to mount an expedition to the Quentas territory? Will you be happy then?"

Her question knifed through him to the center of his heart. "Happy?"

"Yes, content with your life."

Never without you, he thought. But he wasn't worthy of Kate. She was everything good in life—the discovery of the Incan civilization in the Amazon couldn't begin to compare. But she deserved more than he could give her.

"It's late. I need to leave." He skirted her and headed for the door. As he had done in the past when faced with a tough problem, he escaped.

Out on the street he started toward the hotel. Cars sped by. People came out of another apartment building, laughing and talking loudly. *Civilization.*

When he reached the hotel, he kept going. Restless energy propelled him along the sidewalk. He wouldn't be able to sleep even though he had gotten little over the past few weeks. Inside him emotions were shifting, evolving into something he didn't have a handle on. He needed to make sense out of his life, and yet he didn't know where to begin.

At a corner while the stoplight was red, Slader scanned his surroundings as he so often did and saw a church across the street. Lights blazed from it as if it were open even though it was late. When he crossed, he found himself striding toward the church's entrance and into its foyer, surprised that the large, beautifully carved double doors were unlocked. Again he looked around. No one was in the foyer.

The glass doors into the sanctuary beckoned him. It had been years since he had stepped into a church, and yet it felt so right as he pushed open the doors and moved inside. Lights from above highlighted the simple altar at the front.

Slader walked down the middle aisle until he came to the first pew. He sat, folded his hands together in his lap and stared at the cross hanging from the ceiling above the altar. All thoughts flew from his mind for a few seconds, then words began to flood it.

Lord, where do I begin? I feel so lost and alone. How can You ever forgive me for turning my back on You when Renee died? I don't deserve Your love, and yet I'm asking You for it now. I need to feel whole again. I need You back in my life. Please show me the way.

Slader dropped his head until his chin rested on his chest. The quiet in the sanctuary soothed his troubled soul. He thought back to when he had believed in the Lord. Now he realized he had only gone through the motions. He hadn't truly put his life into God's hands. Could he now? Like Kate had in the jungle?

A shuffling sound behind Slader brought his head up. He twisted around and saw an old man making his way toward him. He wore black with a white collar that indicated he was a minister. Slader rose.

"Sit, son." The old man waved him back onto the front pew. "I didn't mean to disturb your time with the Lord. I didn't realize anyone was in here. I only came in to turn off the lights and lock up, but if you need more time, I can give it to you."

Slader slid down the pew to allow room for the minister to sit. The old man settled next to Slader.

"Usually I've locked the church up by now, but…" The minister eyed Slader. "Don't tell anyone I fell asleep in my office. I don't want the congregation to worry about me being alone at the church so late."

"I won't tell anyone."

"You aren't from here, are you, son?"

"No. I've been living in the Amazon for a while now."

"My, you're far from home."

Home. The jungle had never been his home, Slader thought. But where was his home?

"What brought you here tonight?"

Slader rubbed his hand along the back of his neck. "I'm really not sure. I think God did. I mean, I think He led me to this particular place for a reason."

"What's troubling you?"

Where should he begin? Slader thought about his existence for the past five years. That was all he could call what he had been doing—*existing,* until Kate had come into his life. Then everything had changed.

"I walked away from God years ago, and I am here now to see if He will let me return to His fold." The words tumbled from Slader as if someone else controlled what he said. He'd never been one to reveal his problems to others, especially a stranger.

"Did you grow up in the church?"

Slader nodded.

"You've probably heard the story of the prodigal son?"

"Yes."

"Then you know that the Lord has opened His arms wide for you. Whatever is bothering you He can wash away."

Slader stared into the clear blue eyes of the old man.

"Just open yourself up to His love, for it is bountiful, my son."

The minister's raspy voice eased the remnants of his guilt from his soul as if the Lord had indeed washed it away. Emotions, held at bay for so long, crammed Slader's throat, preventing him from saying a word.

"'The fear of man bringeth a snare: but whoso putteth his trust in the Lord shall be safe,'" the old man said as he struggled to stand.

Slader leaped to his feet to help the minister. Placing his arms around the old man, Slader realized how frail he was. "What can I do to help you?"

"Nothing, my son. Your presence is all I need. When a lost sheep returns to the flock, I rejoice. Remember what I said about fear." The man started shuffling toward the back of the sanctuary. "I'll lock the door. Just pull it closed when you decide to leave, and don't worry. Take all the time you need with the Lord." At the glass doors he turned and said, "'For I the Lord thy God will hold thy right hand, saying unto thee, Fear not; I will help thee.'"

With those last words the minister disappeared into the foyer. Slader walked to the step that led to the altar and knelt before it.

"You don't have to hit me over the head, Lord. It's my fear of commitment that is holding me back." He remembered Kate's lack of fear and her strong confidence in God. That was what he wanted in his life. Throwing back his head, he spread his arms wide. "I'm Yours to do as You wish."

Her first day back at work, Kate sat at the back of her church with her fingers laced together in her lap. After having come from her sister's grave site where she'd finally laid to rest her guilt over the fight they'd had the day of the fire, she was ready for the rest of her life—without Slader. Her chest burned whenever she thought of him. It probably always would.

Lord, I'm home for good. I've had my adventure and with Your help survived to tell about it. But Red Creek is where I belong. Thank You for all You've done for me and Zach. We are in Your debt as always. Please watch over Slader and protect him in whatever he does. In Jesus Christ's name, amen.

As she had done over the past few days since returning to Red Creek, Kate wondered where Slader was at that moment. Was he back in Mandras? Was he planning a trip to the Quentas territory to explore the

Incan ruins further? Was he missing her as she was him? There wasn't a second that went by that she didn't ache for him.

She knew all the reasons it wouldn't have worked. He didn't believe in God. He lived thousands of miles away in a self-imposed exile. The two of them were like oil and water, and yet when she thought about their journey in the jungle, she couldn't dismiss the bond that had formed between them. She understood him and strangely she was sure he understood her.

With a sigh, she pushed to her feet and turned to leave. Slader stood a few feet behind her, watching her. When their gazes connected, he smiled, the gleam in his eyes drawing her toward him.

"You're not supposed to be here."

He blinked. "That wasn't quite the reception I had hoped for."

"I was just thinking about you and that you were back in Mandras planning your trip to the Incan ruins."

"Well, I'm glad you were thinking about me, but there isn't going to be an expedition to the Quentas territory. They are one of the last tribes in the Amazon who haven't been exposed to civilization. I want to keep it that way for as long as possible."

"You're passing up excavating those ruins? That was your life's dream."

Slader took a step nearer to her. "That was my old life's dream. My new life's dream is to be with you wherever you want to be. I love you, Kate."

Throat tight, she murmured, "I love you, too."

In two strides he covered the short distance between

them and dragged her against him. "I want a family with you. I want children. I want to live again. Will you marry me, Kate?"

Every thought vanished from her mind. All she could do was stare at him.

"Before you answer, I want you to know that I've changed my mind about God. I want our children to be brought up in the church. We had a long talk that night in Dallas after I left you."

"You talked to God?"

"Yes, and every day since."

Joy showered down on her, bringing forth a bright smile that if it had been dark would have lit the church. "That was three days ago. Where have you been?"

He wound his arms around her and brushed his lips across hers. "I had a debt to pay off, then I needed to make arrangements to support my family."

"What are you going to do? There aren't too many opportunities in Red Creek to be an archaeologist."

"Through some contacts I have, there's an opening for a professor in archaeology at a college just north of Dallas starting the spring semester. Until then, we'll just have to use the time to get to know each other better."

"Will you be going on any digs?"

"Yes, but it can be a family affair if you're willing to have an adventure from time to time. What do you say? Will you marry me, Kate Collier?"

"On one condition."

He quirked a brow. "What?"

"What is your full name? I figure a wife needs to

know that about her husband," she said, although she would always think of him by the name of Slader.

Tossing back his head, he laughed. "My full name is Augustus Cornelius Slader."

EPILOGUE

"Daddy! Look what I found." On short, stubby legs Gus ran toward his father and thrust his hand up into his face.

Slader pried his five-year-old's fist open to discover a pottery shard. "Where did you find this?"

Gus pointed to the underbrush near the archaeological site. "There. My ball rolled under that bush."

"Show me."

Gus took his father's hand and tugged him toward the spot. Slader knelt and pushed the branches away. In the dirt lay several more pieces of white-and-black pottery.

"Well done, son. There might be a whole pot if we dig around some."

"Can I? Can I, Daddy?"

"Of course. This is your discovery." Slader hovered close to make sure Gus didn't damage the pot.

Gus jumped up and down. "Wait until I tell Mommy."

Slader watched his son race toward the tent at the

edge of the site. A few minutes later his son returned dragging his mother behind him.

Slader rose, dusting off his pants. "Our son has found his first piece of pottery." He showed Kate the white-and-black geometrically designed shard.

"It's beautiful." Kate turned it over and examined it from all angles.

"There's my ball." Gus bent and scooped up his red ball, then raced back toward the group of Indian children waiting for him to return.

Slader wiped his sweat-drenched forehead with the back of his hand. "You know, when I lived in the jungle I didn't realize how hot and humid it really was."

"How's it feel to be back after six years?" Kate cuddled up to her husband on the outskirts of the Incan ruins.

"Strange. Exciting. Sad. I had hoped the Quentas would have a little more time before civilization caught up with them."

Kate combed her fingers through his damp hair. "At least you respect their ways and won't exploit them. You were the perfect person to head up this expedition."

"You're all right with returning?"

She chuckled. "Isn't it a little late to be asking me that? We're standing in the middle of a jungle on a plateau that still isn't easy to get to." Standing on tiptoes, she kissed him. "I love you, and I will follow you to the ends of this earth if need be. So yes, I'm all right with this. I want this to be done right and you're the only one I know who will do that."

He cupped her face in his hands. "That's the reason I love you, Kate Slader. You are my biggest fan." He slanted his mouth across hers and proceeded to show her how much he loved her.

* * * * *

Look for Margaret Daley's next book,
SO DARK THE NIGHT,
coming in March 2007,
only from Steeple Hill Love Inspired Suspense.

Dear Reader,

This is my second romantic suspense for the Love Inspired Suspense line, and I have really enjoyed writing it. I loved reading about the Amazon. I immersed myself in the research. I even have a few stories concerning my trek through the jungle—it isn't called a rain forest for nothing. It can really rain a lot. Duh! I discovered that very fact when I ruined a new pair of bright yellow pants because of all the mud I got on them, and I was wearing high rubber boots.

In my story, Slader has to rededicate himself to the Lord. His faith was shaken when his wife died. Sometimes we struggle to keep our faith through the tough times when we feel our prayers have gone unanswered. Kate shows him what faith in the Lord can do for him and becomes a light in the dark for Slader.

I love hearing from readers. You can contact me at P. O. Box 2074, Tulsa, OK 74101 or visit my Web site at www.margaretdaley.com, where you can sign up for my quarterly newsletter.

Best wishes,

Margaret Daley

QUESTIONS FOR DISCUSSION

1. Family was so important to Kate that she traveled to the Amazon to search for her brother when everyone else had given up. What is important to you? Why? Have you put yourself in danger because of it?

2. Slader was racked with guilt over his wife's and unborn child's deaths. He walked away from his life and drowned himself in alcohol. When the numbness of their deaths wore off, he swore off drinking. Have you or a loved one dealt with an addiction of any kind? What has helped you get through it? Did you turn away from the Lord or to Him for help?

3. Slader felt he didn't deserve any happiness. How would you convince him that all people deserve happiness, that God's love is bountiful? What Bible verses would you use to illustrate God's forgiveness?

4. Slader's outlook on life was the opposite of Kate's. She had never faced life's harsh realities, whereas he had—resulting in his cynical outlook. She thought her faith in the Lord would carry her through anything, while he knew that wasn't enough. What is your outlook on life? How have your life experiences shaped it? How has your faith influenced your outlook?

5. We've all heard that opposites attract. Clearly Kate and Slader were opposites. Have you ever loved or cared about a person who is your opposite? What were some difficulties you had to overcome in this relationship because you were so different? Did your faith help you in this?

6. One of the hardest things to do sometimes is to forgive ourselves for something we've done (like Slader). We are often harder on ourselves than others. How can we help to forgive ourselves for something we've done? Why can forgiveness be so hard for a person?

7. Kate was thrown into an alien environment and had to learn to deal with it as the story progressed. Have you ever been thrown into a situation/environment that challenged you? How did you cope? What helped you? Did you rely on your faith? How?

8. Slader had turned away from God in his time of need. Have you ever forgotten God when you needed Him the most? What made you return to the Lord? Was there something that caused you to see the power of God to sustain you in the hard times? A Bible verse?

9. Even though there were people who wanted Kate dead, she couldn't hurt them unnecessarily. When is force necessary? "Thou shalt not kill" is one of the Ten Commandments. How can we justify killing another?

10. Which scene in *Heart of the Amazon* did you like best? Why?

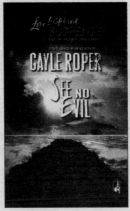

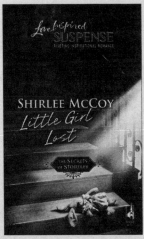

REQUEST YOUR FREE BOOKS!

2 FREE INSPIRATIONAL NOVELS
PLUS 2
FREE
MYSTERY GIFTS

Love Inspired.

YES! Please send me 2 FREE Love Inspired® novels and my 2 FREE mystery gifts. After receiving them, if I don't wish to receive any more books, I can return the shipping statement marked "cancel." If I don't cancel, I will receive 4 brand-new novels every month and be billed just $3.99 per book in the U.S., or $4.74 per book in Canada, plus 25¢ shipping and handling per book and applicable taxes, if any*. That's a savings of 20% off the cover price! I understand that accepting the 2 free books and gifts places me under no obligation to buy anything. I can always return a shipment and cancel at any time. Even if I never buy another book from Steeple Hill, the two free books and gifts are mine to keep forever.

113 IDN EF26   313 IDN EF27

Name	(PLEASE PRINT)	
Address		Apt. #
City	State/Prov.	Zip/Postal Code

Signature (if under 18, a parent or guardian must sign)

Order online at www.LoveInspiredBooks.com

Or mail to Steeple Hill Reader Service™:

IN U.S.A.: P.O. Box 1867, Buffalo, NY 14240-1867
IN CANADA: P.O. Box 609, Fort Erie, Ontario L2A 5X3

Not valid to current Love Inspired subscribers.

Want to try two free books from another series?
Call 1-800-873-8635 or visit www.morefreebooks.com

LIREG07

Love Inspired

PRECIOUS BLESSINGS

BY
JILLIAN HART

Love Inspired®
SUSPENSE

TITLES AVAILABLE NEXT MONTH

Don't miss these four stories in February

SEE NO EVIL by Gayle Roper

Anna Volente discovered a murder *right next door* to the house she was decorating. Now with Gray Edwards, the overprotective owner of the development, hovering and a murderer on her trail, she'll have to rely on her faith to see her through.

LITTLE GIRL LOST by Shirlee McCoy
The Secrets of Stoneley

Someone didn't want Portia Blanchard to find out about her mother. Her investigator was murdered, and Detective Mick Campbell suspected her family. To protect them, she was determined to stick close to the infuriating lawman.

DOUBLE DECEPTION by Terri Reed

After her husband was murdered, Kate Wheeler discovered his double life. Sheriff Brody McClain vowed to help Kate uncover the truth. But the unmasking of the criminal mastermind could destroy Kate's trust—and faith—forever.

A MURDER AMONG FRIENDS by Ramona Richards

The death of her employer turned Maggie Weston's world inside out. She knew a murderer hid among her colleagues and friends. Yet investigator Fletcher MacAllister had his eye on Maggie—as the prime suspect.

LISCNM0107